a songbook of sparks

a songbook of sparks

MARIE BRENNAN

BOOK VIEW CAFE

First published 2025 by Book View Café Publishing Cooperative.
304 S. Jones Blvd. Ste# 2906
Las Vegas, Nevada 89107
http://bookviewcafe.com

Print edition 2025
ISBN 978-1-63632-344-2

"And Ask No Leave of Thee" was first published in *Neither Beginnings Nor Endings*, ed. Richard Fife, April 2022. "Then Bide You There" was originally published in *Dream of Shadows*, July 2022. "Vīs Dēlendī" was originally published in *Uncanny Magazine*, March/April 2019. "What Still Abides" was originally published in *Clockwork Phoenix 4*, ed. Mike Allen, July 2013. "Mad Maudlin" was originally published in *Tor.com*, February 2014. "Cruel Sisters" was originally published in *Daily Science Fiction*, March 2020. "The Twa Corbies" was originally published in *Talebones*, December 2005. "Oh, My Cursed Daughter" was originally published in *Dream of Shadows*, April 2023. "Any Rose My Mother Raised, Any Lane My Father Knows" was originally published in *Frivolous Comma*, August 2024.

Contents

Foreword

There are five basic schools of thought on the topic of author commentary in a short story collection: 1) put it all together at the front; 2) all together at the back; 3) individually before each story; 4) individually after each story; and 5) don't bother.

For the ebook editions of these collections, I can leverage the format to facilitate multiple approaches, by linking to the notes at the end of each story while collecting the notes themselves at the end of the book. Alas, dead trees are not so flexible, which means I have to pick. You will find all the story notes following the Afterword, and can time your reading of them as you choose.

Because I am a notes-after kind of person myself, for now I will say only that this collection contains nine stories (and one bonus poem), all of them based in some fashion on traditional folksongs. They range in length from over seven thousand words to barely five hundred. I hope you enjoy them!

And Ask No Leave of Thee

I'M THE KIND of person who, soon as you tell me not to do something, I do it. Because fuck you, even if you *are* a friend. And Tia wasn't that much of a friend.

So I'm talking about how I'm bored with the Meltdown and there's this old club over on Hall I might check out, and she says I shouldn't because she's heard weird things about what happens to people who go there, and we argue about it a bit until she says—only half-joking—"J, I *forbid* you to go," and that's it: to hell with her. Which I say. So she storms off, and I go home and put on my favorite green skirt, the one I pieced together out of some of Dad's old fatigues, pin it up with some giant safety pins, braid gold LEDs into my hair, and head off to see what this club is like.

I can hear the bass when I'm still two blocks away on Carter. It shakes some of the tension out of my bones. Two weeks this time: two weeks of Dad being home and everything having to be quiet, shhhhh, don't make noise, you know he needs his rest. Meaning the rest of us tie ourselves in knots. Dress nice, don't play that music, no, you can't call Tia, you talk too loud, and why are you always texting? I'm supposed to be happy when my father's around, but the truth is I'm glad he's gone.

No line at the door, which makes me worry, because a club without a line usually isn't worth it. But I walk up to the bouncer with my fake ID in hand.

He doesn't look at it. Doesn't look at me, either, even though I've tugged my shirt down so the neckline's practically at my waist. Just fixes his eye on me and says, "You sure?"

"Yeah, I'm twenty-one," I say, one hand on my hip. He's still not looking. I hate doing this, putting myself out there like a side of meat just so I can get into clubs, but it pisses me off that I'm making the effort and he doesn't care. The look on his face—like he doesn't give a damn whether I'm seventeen or seven or seventy, walking around in my bra or wearing a burka. He just says, "You'll pay before you leave."

I've never heard of a club where the cover charge comes when you leave, but whatever. "Yeah, no problem."

He shrugs—*your funeral, kid*—stamps my hand, and waves me on through.

It's dark inside—so dark I can barely see—but the room is surprisingly crowded for a place with no line at the door. Like all the people cool enough for this club are already here, and nobody else bothers to try. I guess that makes me either special or an idiot: take your pick.

The music is loud enough that it's turned into pure vibration, buzzing through my guts. But there's this melody buried in the buzz, a feral tune that wraps around my spine, and whoever did the acoustics knows their business because I can hear it perfectly. And the people on the floor…it's something about the lights, I think. The strobe flashing makes them look unreal, like they aren't where I think. If I go out there right now, I'm going to slam into somebody, and the mood I'm in, I'll turn it into a fight. Which I kind of want, after two weeks of biting my tongue like a good little girl, but it would suck to get thrown out thirty seconds after I walk in.

So I head for the booze instead. The bar's along the left-hand wall, under some dim lights, and the bartender asks what I want without even giving me the side-eye for being so young. "You got anything special?" I ask. Damn, the acoustics are amazing. I swear the music's as loud as ever, but my voice carries to him just fine.

The bartender's got a weird face, high cheekbones and eyes just a little too big. He gives me the same look the bouncer did— the "your funeral" look. Doesn't say anything, though. Just turns and starts assembling bottles. I watch him the whole time, because I'm not an idiot; I know about roofies. Unless one of the bottles is spiked, what he hands me is clean.

Clean, and red as fresh-spilled blood. "What the hell is this?" I ask, thinking he's given me some stupid fruity girly drink.

"A Rose," he says, which doesn't exactly shout *not girly*. "You wanted the specialty."

I roll my eyes. Whatever. I take the glass and sip my red drink, expecting...

I don't know what I'm expecting, but I get all that and *more*. Sweet, but laced through with bitterness. The taste flowers in my mouth like—well, like a rose, if roses were made of desire and apprehension and forbidden things. And it's alcoholic enough to hit like Dad's fist.

I sway on my stool. For an instant I turn into water, and the music pounds through me, making every part of my body ripple. I open my eyes again and find my sip has turned into a chug: the glass is empty.

"Another?" the bartender asks, and I nod.

This time I'm twitching on my stool, craving a second taste. But just as my hand closes around the glass, somebody else's hand closes on my wrist.

I didn't see the guy come up. Which is a pity, because he's worth looking at. Not hot—not like I'd normally go for—but most nights I'd flip out if a stranger grabbed me like that, and instead I'm just staring. He's Asian, and bony enough that I half-think he's an addict, but on him it looks good. His top is sleeveless and so tight it might as well be painted on. *Magnetic*, that's what he is.

So how did I miss him until he grabbed me?

He says, "I think you've had enough," and his voice carries just as well over the music as mine did.

"I've had *one*," I say. And one is nowhere near enough.

"Why are you here?" he asks. His gaze flicks down for a second, to the stamp on my hand. It's a forked shape, like a peace symbol, or three paths splitting apart: one narrow, one wide, and the one in the middle twisting like a snake.

I laugh. "Why does anybody come to a club? I'm here to have fun." It's a better answer than *I'm here to get fucked up*, even if it's less true. I sink the fingernails of my free hand into his wrist and he lets go, not flinching, releasing me so smoothly I don't spill even a drop of the Rose. I put the rim to my lips, drain the whole thing. It's just as good the second time, waking every nerve in my body.

The burn's still flickering through me when he speaks again, jaw hardening. "You shouldn't be here."

Oh, that is *it*. He isn't even a friend, like Tia. "Fuck you," I say, sliding off my stool. He's taller than I am, but my boots make up a lot of the difference. "Is this your club? No? Then I don't need your goddamned permission. I'll come here any time I like, and leave when I want to."

This close to him, I can feel the heat coming off his body. He's strung tight as a wire, and I recognize that tension: he's looking to get fucked up, too, take whatever's got its claws into him and stomp it into the ground. Maybe he *is* a junkie, twitching for his next fix. Maybe his girlfriend just dumped him for his best friend. Maybe he's got his own shit at home, like me, so he came here to get away from it. Doesn't much matter: we're staring at each other, and damn if I don't think the look in his eyes is recognition, too, one walking time bomb to another.

This time I'm the one who grabs his wrist. He didn't flinch from my fingernails, but he flinches from this. "I can't."

"Fuck that, too," I say, and drag him out onto the floor.

He comes along without another word. When I turn to face him again, he's looking at me like I'm another Rose, something he wants and shouldn't and is going to have anyway. Good for him. Good for both of us. This is a night for doing what we want.

I plant my boots on the sticky floor and drop my hips, looking up at him through my lashes. His shirt is so tight I can see his abs flex as he begins to move. This many people packed in, it ought to be jungle-hot, but the air is cool and crisp as the lights strobing past. We're the only warm things out here. I feel it in my palms when I put them on his hips and grind against him. He stares at me like nothing else exists, and that should be creepy but it isn't, because I feel the same way. All I can see is him.

One of my hands slides along like it's got a mind of its own, over the sharp blade of his shoulder and up to his neck. His hair is stiff with gel, but I bury my fingers in it anyway. The music is spinning my brain around like a top, or maybe that's the Rose; I'm floating out of my body, but I feel every last thing, hyperclear. His hair between my fingers, his belt beneath my other palm, and then his mouth on mine when I draw his head down.

He tastes like the Rose. Maybe I *have* been drugged; everything's hitting sideways. The music is color and movement; dancing is sound; the feel of his lips and tongue is flavor and a guitar pick playing along my bones. His arms go around my back and pull me in, until the only way for us to get closer would be for me to open him up and climb inside.

I don't know which one of us takes the first step toward the back. I just know we're stumbling into a dark and deserted hallway, hands and mouths everywhere at once. He pushes me against a wall and I hike my skirt out of the way, just enough brain left to scrabble at the little pocket until the rubber comes out.

As soon as that's on, everything else vanishes. Half the club could have pushed past us in that hallway and I wouldn't know. There's just him and heat and the music and the dance, pounding together until it all dissolves.

I don't remember paying the bouncer on my way out, but I must have, even though I think I've still got all my cash in my bra the next morning. Did I ever pay the bartender? I can't remember that, either.

Maybe the guy paid him—the one whose name I never learned. God, Tia's going to ask if I went to the club, and I'm a shit liar so I'll have to admit I did, and then she'll want to know what it was like, and what am I going to tell her? I met a guy and fucked him in a back hall. Who was he? Hell if I know.

Thinking it through pulls me up short. Even for me, screwing a total stranger five minutes after I met him is going a little far. Maybe more than a little.

Well, it isn't like I can take it back.

With Dad gone everything's normal at home, Mom snapping at me instead of playing the obedient little Army wife, and even my hangover feels kinda good. When Tia asks, I tell her it's none of her goddamned business what I did last night. The fight we have then feels like the final one, the one that means we aren't friends anymore. I've had enough of those to recognize them when they happen, and they don't hurt much anymore.

Should have been the end of it. I don't exactly regret doing that guy, but once the hangover's gone I have to admit the whole idea was stupid. There's something not right about my memory of that night, like I was tripping as soon as I walked through the door, and how do I know there aren't things I don't remember? I didn't have Tia with me to check against. And now I don't have Tia at all. So I go back to the Meltdown, which is boring but at least I feel safe there. And then one day I go digging in the cabinet below my mom's sink looking for the bag of weed she hid there when Dad came home and find myself staring at the tampons, because how long has it been since I used one of those?

"Mother*fucker*," I say to the tampons. Then I laugh bitterly at my choice of words.

This kind of shit is supposed to happen to the idiots, the girls who think you can't get pregnant if you do it standing up. I always bring a rubber with me. Not that I've had any need for one of *those* lately, either. Not since—

"Mother*fucker*!" I repeat, slamming the cabinet door shut. That goddamned club. The guy whose name I don't know. For one blind moment I think that asshole planned this all somehow—drugged my drink, except I was watching the whole time and roofies can't make sperm swim through a condom. But how much do I remember of that night? The music and the dark hallway and his skin slick-hot against mine. Maybe we did it more than once. Or maybe the fucking thing broke. I wasn't exactly paying attention.

Besides, the *how* doesn't much matter now. I'm goddamned pregnant. And it's about two months too late for the morning-after pill. Which pretty much leaves me making the walk of shame to a clinic, if I can do it without Mom finding out. And Dad—

The chill goes down to my bones. He won't be home again for months, but that'll just give him more time to work himself up, and whether I have a kid or an abortion, he'll be furious. He usually only hits me once or twice, but he won't hold back this time. Or will he throw me out? God, he might. I can't live on the street, with or without a kid.

He might let me stay. Maybe. But the price would be more than I can pay. It won't just be him; it'll be Mom, too. I'll just be a walking reminder that I stopped being a good girl years ago, because if nothing around me is good then why should I bother trying? I'm not the daughter they want, never could be, but Mom glues together a pretty little illusion every time he's home, and this is going to ruin it. They'll never forgive me for that.

But I don't have anywhere else to go. I drove Tia off, like I drive *everybody* off, and now that the chips are down, who do I have?

I climb to my feet, snarling. Okay, it isn't that guy's fault any more than it's mine—I think—and I don't expect any help from him, but I am *damned* if I'm going to be the only one losing my shit over this. And I mean, Jesus. I don't even know his name.

I get dressed like a robot, the same green skirt and gold LEDs, safety pins still where I left them two months ago. He won't have any trouble recognizing me.

And then I go back.

Nothing has changed, except me. It's all the same, the music and the air and the darkness, the people on the dance floor moving in ways people really shouldn't. This might as well be the same night. I wish it *were*, because then I could take back my stupidity.

Since I can't, I look for the guy.

I expect it'll be hard. The lighting makes it impossible to see anybody's face properly, and just because I'm dressed the same doesn't mean he will be, too. With the number of people packed in here, I could spend the whole night searching and miss him.

It takes all of fifteen seconds.

He's standing by a door on the far side of the club, between the bar and the band. There's a little raised platform there, and what do you know, he *is* dressed the same. But he wasn't hoping to find me here tonight. Even with the length of the club between us, I can tell he's glaring at me with the same expression he had when he caught me drinking the Rose.

So I've pissed him off. Good: might as well be two of us.

I'm ready to shove my way through the crowd to him, and never mind the dancers in between. I even start moving, the first step in what's supposed to be an unstoppable rush. But then I *do* stop, flash-frozen where I stand.

The door behind him has opened, and a woman steps out. Somebody's put a light on her or she carries her own light with her, because she's—she's fucking *radiant*, white skin and black hair, red, red lips. Her clothes glitter like a shattered mirror. Something green streams down her back, shreds of fabric, fluttering as she moves.

And he drops. Down on one knee, submissive as a dog. She trails her fingers across his bowed head as she gazes across the club. I wish I could melt into the pillar at my side, because I'm terrified of what'll happen if she sees me, for no good reason at all. It isn't that I think he told her about us. I'm just terrified of *her*. Her beauty's like a knife to my throat. I want to admire it, this woman who obviously doesn't bend for anybody, but the only reason I'm not running is because I'm afraid my knees won't hold me if I move.

She snaps her fingers and he stands, gaze still down. She leans in to whisper in his ear, one hand coming up to cup his jaw. It isn't a lover's touch: I can see her long thumbnail digging into the skin of his neck, green as poison.

It doesn't kill the fear, but the half-formed admiration's gone with a bang. I don't know his name; he's just some guy I fucked in a back hall. But I can't stand seeing him like that—can't stand watching her *own* him like that. All the fire in him is gone, and I know who snuffed it out.

I stumble away, not thinking about where I'm going. The bartender has a Rose on the counter before I even get there. I know damn well I shouldn't drink it, but screw anybody who tells me what to do, even myself. I down the Rose in one go, trying to drown myself in the rush. "Another," I say, need pushing the word out of my mouth. Seeing him up there, kneeling at her feet…like watching Mom knuckle under when Dad comes home. Worse. Because I'm an echo, too, pouring booze down my throat like it's going to solve anything.

"What the *fuck* do you think you're doing?"

His voice takes me by surprise. I figured she wouldn't let him off his leash any time tonight. I reach for my drink, but he grabs my wrist again, and this time the Rose spills, blood all over the floor.

"God damn it!" I snarl. My arm jerks, ready to swing and backhand him across the face.

Only a twitch, nothing more. Because he tenses in response, and I *know* it wouldn't be the first time somebody's done that to him. My throat closes up, sickness rising above the taste of the Rose. My mother's drinking and my father's fists: is that all I've become?

But without those two things, I don't know what to do.

"It's your fucking fault I'm here," I say, and to my horror, it comes out as almost a cry.

His jaw hardens. Maybe he kneels to *her*, but not to me. "You told me you come and go as you please. That you don't need *my* permission."

The last thing I need is my own words thrown back in my face. "I don't mean *here*, you bastard. I mean—I'm fucking *pregnant* because of you."

He goes still. His eyes are so dark they're black, and it makes him look dead for a moment, a corpse puppet whose puppeteer has walked away. I turn away because I can't look at him anymore. The woman's gone, wandered off. Doesn't mean the strings aren't still there.

"Is that why you came here tonight?" he asks. His voice is low, but it carries to my ears, because I swear to god this place makes sound go where it wants. "Is that why you picked the Rose? To kill the child we've made?"

If I'm getting an abortion, I'm going to do it some smarter way than by alcohol poisoning. But I don't say that. "I don't know why I came. There's no point, is there? It isn't like you're going to help me. You *can't*." He's trapped worse than I am.

The silence seems to go on forever. How can it be so quiet where the two of us are standing, when all around us the music is shaking the air? Finally I can't take it anymore and turn to look at him.

The sight hits me harder than the Rose did. Because I expected anger, desperation, despair.

His eyes are full of hope.

It isn't the dance floor he drags me to. We go to a back hall, the same place where we fucked, I think, so far as I can remember it. It actually *is* quieter back here, even though I can still see out onto the floor, like somebody's put a layer of muffling between us and the speakers. He stands close anyway, close enough that he has to tilt his face down or be talking over my head. I can either crane my neck, or stare at his shoulder. I pick the shoulder, even though it distracts me with a fragmentary memory of biting the smooth skin there.

"I'll help you," he says. "But you have to help me first."

I plant both hands on his chest and shove him back a step. "Fuck you. First you do this to me; then you have the *balls*—"

"It isn't fair," he says readily. "I know that. But it's the best I can do. If you can get me away from her, I can help you. I *will*."

"Fine. Let's go. There's got to be a back door around here somewhere."

He puts out one hand to stop me. "It isn't that easy."

If it were, he would have walked away already. "What do you need? A place to stay?" Not my house, that's for damn sure. Not even with Dad gone. I wonder whether I could talk Tia into it, or whether I've burned that bridge too thoroughly.

"Midnight tomorrow," he says, "I'm going to die."

Everything drops away. The hallway, the music, the whole damned club, everything except him. He isn't kidding.

Midnight.

Dead.

"She's going to kill you," I say. My voice sounds like it belongs to somebody else.

The world comes back. He moves his head in something that might be a nod or a shake—like there isn't much difference between yes and no. "I'm going to die for her," he says. "Because of her. She's got it planned."

"What is she, a gang leader?"

His shoulders jerk. I'm not sure if it's a laugh. "Something like that. She's throwing me to the wolves. To keep herself safe. Herself and her people."

So he's not one of her people? No, of course not. I've seen her people on the dance floor, wild and cold. I shake myself, trying to clear my head of the Rose's fog. She's—what, selling him out to another gang? Or to the police? Yeah, I could see that. "So I'm just fucked. Metaphorically."

He hesitates, and goddammit, now I'm feeling something like hope, too. I want to have *some* option other than being stuck with this all by myself. "What?"

His voice drops until I can barely hear it, even with this place's weird acoustics. "We both are. Unless we help each other."

"How the hell am I supposed to help you?"

My words make his mouth twist in the most painful smile I've ever seen. He says, "Be there tomorrow night, at the intersection of Miles and Cross. Claim me as your own. You can do that now—if you want to."

Now, but not before. Because I'm pregnant? "You really think these wolves she's throwing you to will care if I say, don't kill him, I'm carrying his kid?"

He just looks at me. Waiting.

Well, fuck. If I were in his place, I'd think it was true, too. Because that's better than dying without hope.

I've never been what you'd call cautious, but the question still comes out of my mouth: "Will it be dangerous for me?"

His answer is faint, barely more than a breath. "Yes."

Of course. So now it's all on me: here you go, J, you've got this guy's life in your hands, and also a life in your belly, oh and let's not forget about your own, and you've got until tomorrow night to decide how many of those you're going to bet on black.

"Why the fuck should I help you?"

His mouth twists to one side in a pained, self-mocking grin. I know that grin. I know what it feels like from the inside. "If my impending death isn't enough to convince you, I don't know what would be."

"Tell me what's going on. Who she is. How you ended up like this. Tell me you don't deserve it, that you're just an innocent bystander." But he isn't. I knew that as soon as I saw him at her heels. There's no innocence in this place, unless it rode here inside me tonight.

He could lie, and maybe I'd let him, because at least a lie would give me something to hold onto. Instead he just says, "I made a stupid fucking mistake, and she got me. Seven years she's had me, and tomorrow night it ends. I go with you, or I go to Hell."

The way he says it is different. I've told people to go to hell often enough, but I never meant it like he does. I glance out at the dance floor and the place seems to get darker, the music more desperate. Like they're all dancing to distract themselves from the pit gaping below.

It's a dumb move, but I cast my gaze around, looking for her. Looking *at* her—there's no need to search. She's clear on the other side of the club, but I can see every detail, every flash of light from her body when she laughs. A queen on her throne. Just the sight of her is a declaration: *Everything here is mine, and you have nothing. You have only what I permit you.*

Just like my father, when he's home.

So fuck her. And fuck her plans.

"What do you need me to do?"

⁂

It's goddamned cold at the ass-end of October, and all the street-lights along Miles Avenue are burned out. This is sketchy fucking territory, even for me. I'm convinced I'll get mugged or murdered before I even make it to the intersection.

But I don't see a soul the whole way there. It's near the club—just a few blocks down Hall—which means this is probably her turf. And I guess everybody here knows when to clear out. Unlike me.

My boots crunch bits of broken glass along the sidewalk, and then I'm at the intersection, with the stoplights glaring red and green overhead. I hang close to the wall and scope the place out, looking for her people, him, the cops, or whoever. But there's nobody. And it crosses my mind that maybe this is some kind of asshole trick, luring me out here so they can all have a big laugh, or worse.

No. He didn't make this up. That much, I'm sure of.

I find a good doorway to lurk in and hunch my shoulders inside my old green hoodie, hands fisted in the pockets. My boots are a reassuring weight on my feet. He didn't say anything about me needing to fight, but the steel toes make me feel better all the same.

Fuck. I *still* don't know his name.

And maybe I never will, because the minutes drag by and nobody shows up. I don't even know what I'm doing out here. But every time I think about going home, the stubbornness kicks in, and then I just wish there was somebody here for me to stomp.

The nearest streetlight flicks to green, then back to red, and it starts blinking. Midnight.

In the distance, I hear the growl of engines.

Headlights coming down the street, single beams with odd spacing. Motorcycles, not cars. I press myself deeper into the shadow, watching them come closer. One bike is out in front, and no prize for guessing who's on *that* one.

I can't even look at her. The bike's a monster, black and lethal, but she controls it with a careless hand, hair streaming behind her like whips. Her arms are bare, inked with barbed wire, winding around the lean muscles and vanishing at her shoulders. That's as far as my eyes will go before flinching away. Behind her come others, a whole crowd of them on a crowd of different machines, none of them black because they aren't fucking stupid enough to compete with *her*.

Last of all, him.

His bike is white and it shines like the moon in the darkness. *He* shines. Bright enough for me to see the blood on his knuckles, his left sleeve torn off—they've put him in white leathers for this, but not without a fight. He's got a helmet on, somebody's idea of a fucking joke, but the visor's up and I can see his eyes in the gap, staring straight ahead, too desperate to look around for me. Maybe he's afraid that if he does, she'll know. Or maybe he's afraid I'm not here.

Doesn't matter what the fear is. It's there, and it punches me under the ribs, knocking all my air away. No time to wait and catch my breath, though. I know what I have to do.

His bike hasn't even passed when I run into the street, clamp my hand on his collar and drag him off the bike.

I have all the time in the world to watch it happen: my fingers curling into the fabric, the jerk as his body slows and the bike keeps going forward. The sideways wrench of me hauling him to the pavement. The bike rolling on a few yards more before it falls.

Every bike in front of us wheeling around like the riders knew this was coming, right down to the instant.

And blue and red light splitting the air, dancing a siren song on the walls around us.

Fuck.

So there I am: standing over him on the asphalt, hands in fists, ready to punch anybody who comes near. And there she is: her bike purring through the rest and stopping at the edge of the ring. Red and blue light twisting the whole scene, the cops on their way, but they aren't here yet, so maybe I still have a chance.

And she says, "You would claim what belongs to me?"

I can't spit far enough to hit her, but I do my best. "If he belonged to you, you wouldn't sell him out like this."

Her laugh cuts like broken glass. "If he did not, he would not be mine to sell. Claim him or be gone."

Right, like anybody's going to let me walk out of here if I say oh, shit, I'm having second thoughts. He's quiet on the ground between my feet, not even twitching; if it weren't for that helmet I'd be afraid I'd knocked him out. It's the quiet of helplessness: whatever's going to happen now is up to me.

And she's so fucking *sure* of herself. Like it's been so long since anybody challenged her, she can't remember what it's like.

I'm going to remind her.

"Yeah," I say. "He's mine. That goes for you assholes, too," I say to the cops closing in, remembering too late that my story might go over better if I didn't insult them. "He's not part of this. She tried to lure him in, but it isn't his fault. She's the one you want, and he can give you proof. I swear it."

I'm making this shit up as I go, which means it isn't my best lie ever. Her lips pull back in a smile like a snake eyeballing which vein it wants to go for. "Opening with a falsehood? You are lost before you begin."

I am; I can feel it. The cops will take me along with him, and I don't know whether that means jail or a bullet in my brain. "Fine," I say. "You want truth? Let's try this one. You're a bitch. An evil, bloodsucking, soulless bitch, and you're selling him out to save your own skin. But he's *mine*, not yours. I've got his kid in me, and I am fucking well going to make him stick around and deal with that. And I will kick in the face of anybody who tries to get in my way."

I don't expect mercy, and I don't get it. The cops stop moving— they're just shadows at the corners of my vision, hovering, barely visible past *her*. Silhouettes against the red and blue light. But she cocks her head to one side, still smiling, and says, "Are you so certain you want him? You do not even know what it is that you claim."

Smooth as blood flowing from a cut, he slides out from between my feet and stands up.

His right glove is gone now, too, and his hands are so stiff the tendons and bone stand out like sticks. They reach up and pull the helmet from his head. He stands there, holding it, until she says, "Tell her."

She's still his puppeteer, dragging his head up and making him look me in the eye. He meets my gaze and says, "She's right. You don't know me."

I force myself to shrug. "That didn't stop me from fucking you in a back hall. Why should it stop me now?"

"Because I'm a thief," he says. "I've gone into people's homes, mugged them on the streets. I broke a man's legs with a crowbar, not because he hadn't paid a debt, but because I knew he hadn't given me everything he had. I took a woman's child, then forced her to pay all she could afford and more to get that child back."

It isn't just words. I can see it in him, see echoes of it around him, like those other riders and the cops are acting it out at the edges of my vision, though that's fucking crazy and I'm pretty sure I'm hallucinating out of stress. He's telling the truth.

But he's already told me he isn't an innocent. "So what," I say, trying to make it sound casual. "I've stolen things, too. Not from people's houses, but it isn't like I can really throw stones. You're still mine."

He grins, wolfish and sharp. "Still yours. Even though I'm a killer." He flings the helmet away. The crack of it hitting the pavement makes me jump, and in that instant he's there, knife at my neck, and if I so much as breathe too hard it'll cut me. His gaze burns like fire, barely three inches away. "I've killed in her name, at her command. I've cut men's throats, shot them while they fled, beaten them to death with my own hands. And though I acted at her word, the pleasure I took in it wasn't hers. It was my own."

The blood is there, filling my vision, the screams of his victims echoing around us. I've broken a guy's nose before, but I've never kept beating him when he's crawling on the ground, too shattered to stand. I've threatened to use a knife on somebody, but I've never followed through.

My own blood is hammering in my ears. I don't know why he's doing this, except she wants him to, and that means she wants me to give up. But even if I end up regretting it later, the whole reason I came out here tonight was to shove my thumb in her eye. I swallow, a faint line of fire tracing my throat where that makes the knife bite down, and I say, with every bit of certainty I can scrape together, "You won't kill me. And I'm taking you with me when I leave."

The knife drops to the ground. His hand slides up my throat, around to the back of my neck. *He* slides around, circling behind me, calling up memories of the night we danced, the night we fucked—and then his arm clamps down, pinning mine, and his free hand shoves between my legs. I'm still wearing the same skirt, I guess out of superstition, like it's going to bring me good luck. Instead it brings me this: his fingers forcing themselves into me, and it isn't hot at all, it's a violation, and I hear him laugh softly in my ear.

"You're taking me with you? On the basis of one single night. One drunken fuck in a darkened hall. You can't even explain to yourself why you did it, can you—can't understand why the condom failed, why you're pregnant. And then this poor, tormented soul says he needs you, you and your child, you're the only thing that can save him.

"But did you think to ask why? Or whether you're the first? Do you have any idea how many girls I've taken in that hallway— girls so drunk, so *high* on the Rose, they would have spread their legs for every creature in that club. It's a *game*, don't you see. And you fell for it."

I can't breathe. I watched so closely—but I thought about it, didn't I, that watching wouldn't be enough if one of the bottles was spiked already. The Rose, the plucked blossom; I was no virgin, long before I came to that club, but the joke's there all the same. Deflowered. He's hard against my ass, his hand violating me in front of all these people…

And she's right in the middle. Watching. Laughing.

The taste of the Rose blooms again in my mouth, and I *see.*

The barbed wire climbing her arms turns into a thorny vine, pricking her skin so the blood trails down in dark curves. The collar of her top climbs upward and out, feathers and leaves, flaring in a suggestion of wings. Her clothing is a live thing, branches and serpents and the skins of creatures that aren't quite dead, wild and horrifying in its beauty. *She* is horrifying. Inhumanly perfect—because she is not human.

Behind her, all the others of her court, some like animals, others like trees, all the creatures that fit that place, the club I could never properly see. They hiss and howl, watching me, feral in their eager-ness, waiting to see how this will end.

And beyond them, the cops....

The blue and red lights smear into flame, ringing us in this place that is no longer a street. I can only see the figures as black hollows against that light and I'm glad of it, because they're not human either, and if I saw *these* creatures headon, my mind would be in pieces on the ground.

I go with you, or I go to Hell.

He meant it literally.

My breath comes in a ragged gasp and I see both worlds, over-laid on each other, melding and slipping apart: the ordinary world, where a gang stands in the street with a ring of cops closing in around them, and this other place.

Where the Queen of Faerie stands ready to sell a mortal man to Hell.

And I can feel his heart, thudding too fast against my back. It isn't arousal. It's terror. Shrieking, desperate, animal terror. She's making him do this, transform himself in my eyes, turning himself into every kind of monster. Trying to make me let go of him. And I can't tell whether it's all some kind of trick, whether the words coming out of his mouth are lies after all or the truth I don't want to hear. Maybe he *did* do all of those things. Maybe he did kidnap children, beat men to death, drug and rape girls in a back hallway. I don't know.

But I do know one thing. If I let him drive me away, then I

know exactly where he's headed.

Go to hell, I've said, a thousand, thousand times.

Those words will never come out of my mouth again.

"Nobody fucking tells me what to do," I say, wrenching one arm free and grabbing his wrist, digging my nails in hard. "Including you. I pulled you out onto that floor, I asked for the Rose—and *I'm not letting you go.*"

Sirens split the air, pounding me like clubs to the head, and then the gunfire starts.

I drag him sideways, out of the middle of the street, back down the dark length of Miles Avenue. His white clothes are too goddamned conspicuous; I yank off my hoodie, shove him into it, too small but at least it's better, and then we run.

Off Miles, into streets I know better, streets with their lights still on, back into the human world. It feels solid and real and I could drop right there to kiss the pavement. But we've got to go somewhere, and it can't be my house, and it can't be the club. So where?

When he can speak, he says, "I don't know if she's ever failed before. I don't know what they'll do to her."

The legions of Hell. My skin shudders like it's trying to crawl right off me. "Couldn't happen to a nicer bitch."

He slows, stops, and since I don't want to let go of his hand I stop, too. He bites his lip, looks away. Says, "The things I said were true. Partly."

He's a thief and a killer. And maybe I wasn't the first girl to drink the Rose, to go with him into that back hall.

But it's only *partly* true. And that means it isn't as bad as he made it sound.

It's still pretty fucking bad.

I wonder whether telling him to take a hike now will mean Hell gets him after all. Or the cops. But you know, I don't really want to.

Not yet. I don't want to end up like Mom, shackled to someone who really isn't worth it, and maybe this guy isn't worth it, either. Or maybe I'm the one who isn't. But for once in my life, I want to think something through before I make up my mind. Get to know the guy before I decide whether I want him in my life or out of it.

"I'm J," I say, looking in his dark, bruised eyes. "Janet, really. But if you ever call me that, I'll kick you in the shins."

The night is quiet enough that I hear his breath waver as he draws it in. "Tam," he says, hand tightening on mine. "Tam Lin."

We're on Tia's street. I don't have a lot of experience with mending bridges…but you only learn by trying. "Nice to meet you, Tam. Come on—my friend's house is on the corner."

Then Bide You There

THAT AFTERNOON there had been a fair, with jugglers and dancing and the storyteller plying her trade. When night fell the fair did not end, but the storyteller was tired, and the blacksmith insisted on walking her home.

"They give up too easily," he said as she unlatched her front door.

"Who?"

"The gods. In your tales. The lady turns into a tree or a flower or a star in the sky, and the god simply walks away. If I were a god, I would not abandon the chase so easily."

She paused, one hand on the latch. "No. Clearly you would not."

He kept talking as she went inside, as she stirred up the banked fire, found an ember, lit a spill and then the lamps. How he would become a bird and nest in the tree, a bee and pollinate the flower, a cloud and envelop the star. He said, "There is always a way—for a determined man."

She poured wine for herself. He took down another cup and poured as well. She said, "So if I were to make myself a single grain in a field of wheat…"

"Easily done. I would turn into a swarm of locusts and devour every last seed." He lifted the cup and drank deep, then filled it a second time. "You are a clever woman, but I am more clever still."

"And if I became a stick of kindling, buried deep in the wood-pile of your forge?"

"You are far too proud to come near my forge—as I know all too well. But if you did, I would be the fire that consumed the pile, kindling and log entire.”

"Then if I were a rat, fleeing the fire, and hid among your chickens.”

“A nimble and fine-furred rat you would make. I would be a fox, even nimbler and finer of fur, and sharp of tooth. I would tear and tear until I caught you.”

He had torn and torn for years, and not just at her. But he had not caught her yet. "What if I became a hair on the back of your old dog?”

"That vicious thing?” The blacksmith laughed. “I would skin him and lay his hide on my bed. It would be the only good service he’s ever done, and you would keep me warm.”

“And if I should become a hole in the ground?”

He leaned in closer, his breath rank with more than just wine. "I would lay me in that hole. In the end, even your pride cannot deny me your embrace.”

The storyteller smiled and said, "Then bide you there forevermore.”

As dawn broke the next day, the buzz of locusts hushed over the field, and the light of the burning forge died down into ash. No chickens scratched, nor dog barked. And the ground outside the storyteller’s house lay quiet beneath her feet as she went to fetch water from the well.

Vīs Dēlendī

THE MASTERS FILE into the high-vaulted chamber with its ceiling of clear, faceted crystal. The rainbow light cast by the sun finds its echo in their robes, fine silks in all the shades of their titles: sky-blue, steel-grey, rose-red, blood-red. The thrones upon which they seat themselves are carved from impossibly large blocks of the stones for which they are named. Kings covet thrones as fine as these, but anyone who thinks to conquer this place and take them as a prize will soon have a thousand reasons to regret his error.

In the center sits the Opal Master, resplendent and stern. Without a single sweep of her hand she raises the wards that will shield this room from sight and sound; they mute the light from the crystal ceiling, and in the gloom the Masters and their thrones glow all the more vividly.

She declares the thirteen convened, and the most junior among them, the Turquoise Master, asks the first question. "Who stands before us?"

The words are ritual. For weeks the halls of the academy have echoed with whispers, rumors and speculations and more than a few wagers. Everyone knows *who*. Everyone knows *why*. But no one knows *what*—or how it will play out.

He steps forward, wearing the undyed muslin of a candidate, and halts on the block of dull granite that marks the center of the floor. "I am Harrik Neconnu, and I stand before the Masters."

"For what purpose do you come before us?" Jasper, second most junior. The more interesting questions are reserved for the senior Masters.

"I come before you to submit myself for examination."

Now comes the first chance for something unexpected, with the question of the Lapis Master. "What degree do you seek?"

"I seek the degree of *vīs faciendī*."

A soft rustle of silk, as the Masters shift in their seats.

They are not surprised. To achieve the degree of *vīs sciendī* requires examination by only three Masters, and *vīs mūtandī* requires seven. They would not be here, all thirteen of them, if they had not known how Neconnu would answer.

But still: ambition is always noteworthy. *Vīs faciendī* is the most difficult of the three degrees, and the most rarely bestowed.

The Hematite Master says, "Do you understand that if you fail this test, you will be put out of the academy, and not permitted to return?"

"I do."

He is not a remarkable student, Neconnu. Some among more senior Masters—those not required to take on teaching duties—did not even recognize his name when they found it entered into the lists for examination. But this is not as unusual as one might think; magi are not known for their humility. Already this year three candidates have overreached themselves, and been sent away.

Odds are high that Neconnu will be the fourth. But he must have his chance.

The Obsidian Master asks the question that pulses behind every serene expression. "What act will you perform, to prove your right to the degree of *vīs faciendī*?"

Harrik Neconnu says, "I am going to return the dead to life."

He isn't the first to try.

Countless magi, hoping to earn the highest of the three degrees, have turned to myths and legends for inspiration. In stories great heroes have brought the sun to a halt, traveled backward in time, transformed themselves into stars in the sky; why should it not be possible for magi to do the same? They command the forces of existence. Surely nothing is beyond their reach.

And sometimes they are correct. The academy cultivates such hubris because from time to time it produces results; some of the invocations that now form part of the standard examination for *vīs sciendī* were once the means by which someone earned the degree of *vīs faciendī*, in the early days when the academy was new and few forms of magic were known.

But resurrecting the dead…that, no one has yet achieved. Invoking ghosts, yes. Raising corpses as shambling puppets, yes.

A true return to life?

That has always remained out of reach.

The Masters relax on their thrones. No one laughs, or even smiles; they have too much dignity and self-control for that. But now they know how exactly to classify the young man in front of them: a mediocre student, his ambition far in excess of his skill, hoping to make his name in one dramatic stroke. *Vīs faciendī* means a guaranteed position among their ranks in due course, once a seat becomes available; the Alabaster and Opal Masters both earned their titles that way. But this foolish boy is unlikely to join them.

The Carnelian Master is not quite as well-controlled as the rest. A hint of indulgent amusement creeps into his voice as he says, "Where do you intend to perform this act? We have no body here for you to raise."

"We will have to leave this room," Neconnu says. "My method requires us to visit the grave."

There is precedent. Although the examinations for all three degrees are customarily conducted in secrecy, some effects cannot be performed in the confines of this chamber. The Opal Master earned her degree on the rocky crag that rears up behind the academy's halls, splitting the heavens with the lightning into which she had transformed her body.

"What tools will you need?" the Agate Master asks.

"None."

This time he *has* surprised them. There are things a magus can do without needing material assistance from herbs or candles, bells or diagrams, feathers or the stones for which the Masters are named. But most of them are smaller effects, simple matters like manipulating objects at a distance or conjuring water or fire. Greater things can still be done unaided, as the Opal Master demonstrated in raising the wards, but this requires great skill and power; she holds the degree of *vīs mūtandī* as well as *vīs faciendī*. An unremarkable student like Neconnu is unlikely to be capable of any such thing.

The traditions of this examination allot only one question to each Master, but Agate cannot hold back from saying more. Not bothering to hide his skepticism, he says, "You expect us to believe you can raise the dead by will alone?"

"No," Neconnu says. "But the one thing I need, I hold within myself."

This is more plausible. Blood, breath, hair, flesh—the components of the body have countless uses in a magus's work. To achieve something as significant as restoring the dead to life without a great array of paraphernalia seems unlikely…but others have brought in wagonloads full of tools and still failed. Perhaps the answer will turn out to lie in simplicity after all.

They return to the questions, with Chrysoprase leaning forward in her curiosity. "How much time do you need to prepare?"

"None," he says again. "I have already begun."

Something about him irks them all, and has done so ever since he entered the room. Perhaps it is the arrogance with which he stands there, this mediocre student, so unremarkable in his classes that half of them could not have named him or even known him for one of their own. He does not smile, any more than the Masters do, but they can all see him *not* smiling, as if he is too magnanimous to gloat over the accolade he has not yet earned…but not so magnanimous that he doesn't want them to know that he is holding back.

And their irritation finds just cause in that reply. Each Master has only one question to ask, but free rein to condemn the answers they receive. Chrysoprase slaps one palm against the arm of her throne, blue-green as the shallow sea and carved with intricate knots. "I deny the degree. You condemn yourself from your own mouth: we must see you demonstrate the power of creation in order to judge it. To begin without us is trickery."

Neconnu bends his head, graciously but without apology. "There is precedent. Two hundred years ago Ajan Eixt earned the degree of *vīs faciendī* by causing a severed limb to regrow, despite having begun before the examination, because his working began by accident."

This reply creates an opening for Alabaster, who alone among the Masters does not have his words dictated by ritual. His role is to ask the question that cannot be planned for, because it is unique to the circumstances at hand. Now he tilts a measuring gaze at Neconnu and says, "Do you claim yours began by accident as well?"

Neconnu's path would be smoother if he says *yes*. But the magi who seek the highest degree are even less known for their humility than their lesser brethren. He says, "No. I name Eixt only to show that there is precedent. I began my working in full knowledge of what I was doing…but had I told anyone at the time, it would have ruined the attempt."

"Explain," Alabaster says. Commands are not questions.

Neconnu hesitates for just an instant. But here in this room he has no liberty; he must answer the questions and obey the commands of the Masters, or suffer consequences far worse than expulsion. He says, "My working relies on…intent. Not only my own, but in a sense, that of those around me. For them to know what I am doing would affect their responses, and thus risk destroying what I seek to create."

A pause as the Masters consider. Then Neconnu speaks again, without being bidden. "You will understand when you see my working. And I am sure that when you do, you will judge that I too had sufficient cause for beginning before I entered this room."

The collective intake of breath around the room says that more than a few of the Masters are less certain than he. But when

Alabaster looks to Opal, she nods. And so the ritual continues on, to the Sardonyx Master.

He says, "How long will you need to…complete your working?"

The word is supposed to be "perform." But Neconnu has already begun, and Sardonyx judges it more important to ask the correct question than to adhere to the precise phrasing.

Now a hint of the smile begins to show through, as if Neconnu cannot hold it back any longer. He answers both the question asked, and the one it should have been. "My working has been in progress for one year. Today it will conclude, and once we reach the grave, that should take no more than a few minutes."

A year and a day! Half the Masters look to their leader, as Alabaster did a moment before. They have never heard of a working that takes so long, but if anyone among them has, it will be the Opal Master.

She, however, does not meet anyone's gaze. She is rigid on her throne, the shifting colors of her robe lending the illusion of movement, but the woman herself is as still as death.

Malachite, failing to realize the significance, asks his question. "Who is the target of your working, that you intend to raise from the dead?"

The smile breaks free, beatific and smug.

Neconnu says, "Voland Eleir."

Voland Eleir!

The Masters need no reminder of *her* name. She is known to them all, and even those who disliked her on personal grounds could not deny her potential. At first they shrugged it off as the advantage of her birth and upbringing, giving her an early start compared to her fellow students. But as time passed and others showed their promise, Voland kept ahead of them all. She did not merely possess talent; she had dedication, determination, the will to apply herself to her studies and the intelligence to see how they could be taken further. *Vīs sciendī* would surely be a mere formality, for her memory was prodigious. *Vīs mūtandī*, a certainty, for she had the knack of adapting known magic to variant ends. *Vīs faciendī*… If anyone in this generation could earn that degree, surely it would be Voland Eleir.

It broke their hearts when she died.

A year and a day, since the accident that claimed her life. One of the senior students, ambitious to earn the degree of *vīs mūtandī*, experimented with the Opal Master's achievement, seeking to transform himself into flame instead of lightning. His most successful attempt failed to achieve any change in his own body; he only created a firestorm that burned Voland to bone on the spot.

They can heal, the magi of the academy. The first bestowment of *vīs faciendī* was for that discovery. But no power can restore life once it has fled, and so the brightest star of the next generation was snuffed out like a mere candle.

He is gone now, the student who killed her. Not just exiled, but the spark of his power torn out of him so he can use it to harm no more. Not that it does any good. It won't restore Voland Eleir to them.

If Neconnu can do what he says, though…that star will shine again.

And the Opal Master will have her granddaughter back.

"How?"

The Opal Master is on her feet, hands rigid as stone. That final question properly belongs to the Jade Master, but no one begrudges her this break in ritual. It is no secret that the current Opal dreamt of her granddaughter someday occupying the same throne. Whether Neconnu can return Voland to the world of the living or not, he has already brought life where it has not been seen for a year and a day: the Opal Master blazes with all the bright fire of her namesake, after twelve months of cold resignation to her duty.

They can feel his satisfaction. A mediocre student? He has their attention now; none among them will ever forget his name again. Whether they will remember him for his success or for his failure is a different matter, of course…but he shows not the slightest flicker of uncertainty. Neconnu has labored for the last year to bring about this end. If he were susceptible to doubt, he would not have made it this far.

He tips a bow toward the Opal Master, shallower than it should be, but her mind is on matters other than etiquette. "Accompany me to her grave," he says, "and I will tell you."

No eyes see them go. These examinations are not public spectacles, to be witnessed by all the students and servants of the academy; they are not for entertainment. No one outside the thirteen Masters and one candidate will know anything of what transpires until after it is done.

The Opal Master does not maintain the wards that hide them. The Jade Master does that for her, without question or complaint.

Voland's grave lies to the south. In theory this cemetery is only for those who have earned a degree, and she had none. But a unanimous vote of the Masters held that, although she was never examined for *vīs sciendī*, she had demonstrated all the knowledge necessary and more; they awarded her the degree posthumously. A thing never done before in the history of the academy, but those who complained had enough sense to do so quietly.

The Opal Master would not accept her granddaughter being buried in the unmarked grave of a student who fell short.

Her headstone is a simple one, carved only with her name, her posthumous degree, and the emblem of the academy, a thirteen-pointed star. Neconnu approaches it, and the Opal Master's breath hisses between her teeth as he lays a familiar hand on the stone, smiling down at Voland's name. His expression manages to convey sadness and anticipation, all at once.

He says, "Do you remember the tale of the Maiden of Sorrow and Joy?"

Some of them do not, and their brows furrow as they try to place the reference. Some do, and their brows furrow as they scowl.

The twelve questions have been asked, and they have left the chamber; ritual does not bind their words now. Lapis snorts. "A *folktale?*"

Neconnu's smile remains unchanged. "Her wicked suitor struck down her true love on the first day of spring. She begged for a year in which to mourn, before he brought her to the circle for marriage, and he granted it to her."

Now the others remember. It is a story told to children: how the Maiden of Sorrow and Joy went to her lover's grave every day and wept for her loss, through the summer, the autumn, the long nights of winter, in which her tears froze like diamonds on her lips.

He claimed he began his working a year ago. Alabaster says, "You have been mourning Voland all this time?"

Malachite scoffs. "Foolishness. This is not any true invocation; crying cannot raise the dead. If it could, no loved one would ever be lost."

Neconnu's fingers whiten against the stone. "It is not mere *crying*. Only the truest grief will suffice, and it must be sustained, without fail. Only I had the dedication to do this for her. Only I loved her enough."

The Opal Master is torn between hope and fury. "Do you suggest I did not love my granddaughter?"

"You asked how my working has been and will be performed," Neconnu says. "This is how."

At first it was easy. He had only to cast his thoughts on Voland for the tears to come. In those days he was not the only one who wept…but he visited her grave in secret, because alone among the students and Masters at the academy, he grieved with purpose. And, as he would tell the Masters when he came before them on his examination day, for others to know that purpose might ruin its intent.

Wherein lay his challenge. He must mourn Voland, while at the same time hoping for her return.

During her life he had written her poems. He reread these obsessively, sinking his mind into the passion of the past, contrasting it with the hollow emptiness of the present. When those lost their power to move him, he wrote new poems, tormenting himself with the thought that their object was gone. He counted every day since her death as a day in which he could not behold her beauty, another day before he could caress her smooth skin and kiss her flawless mouth. He wept for the absence of Voland from his life.

He rationed out his grief with care. Each memento he had of her was brought out in turn—a note in her hand, a ribbon with her scent—and studied, kissed, clutched to his breast as he huddled in the shelter of her headstone, until use rendered it too familiar, the note smudged, the ribbon frayed. He lamented that he had not more relics to remember her by, and used that lack to flagellate himself into a few days more of tears.

By such means did the months roll by…but there were months yet to go.

He set out to collect more relics of Voland. Those who held them did not value them, did not value *her*; they had moved on from their grief, revisiting it from time to time, but not making their home within it as he did. A beloved book, a dried wreath of flowers, a scarf loaned to a friend. An opal pendant, a gift from her grandmother. No one would begrudge those things if they knew why he took them—and if they did, why, then they were no true friends to Voland, but traitors who would abandon her to the cold embrace of the grave.

The hardest part was to grieve alone. His solitude was fuel for a time—proof that even in life, she had not been loved as she deserved—but as the year of mourning drew on, he knew he needed aid. And yet he could not explain his working to anyone, or their own hope might destroy his chance.

So he found ways to remind them of what they had lost.

Her favorite song, hummed under his breath, so that a friend picked up the melody without realizing, then wept at the memory. Those tears did him no good—they were not shed on Voland's grave, and the friend had ceased her daily sobbing months before—

but the sight of another's grief freshened his own.

A tome laid open at the very spot in the library where she was wont to sit. A half-eaten apple left on the sunny stone where she used to meditate. He knew her writing by heart, and so he copied the style of her hand, slipping messages under pillows or between the pages of books, until rumors spread among the students of a haunting. The robe he had reclaimed served good purpose, when paired with a wig of black horsehair and a simple illusion; people began to swear they had seen her ghost.

Until one of the senior students caught him. That one beat him without mercy, accusing him of cruelty, malice, tormenting everyone for no better reason than ill will.

He did not try to argue or explain. Being misunderstood served his purpose, and so did the pain. He submitted to the beating, then killed the senior student before any whisper of his activities could reach someone else's ears. That night he dragged himself to Voland's grave and wept more easily than he had in weeks, even as he knew his triumph was near.

A year and a day. He could suffer that long for her sake, knowing that in the end, they would be together at last.

A blast of wind slams Neconnu against the headstone, holding him pinned.

"*You,*" the Opal Master snarls, her fury breaking loose at last. "You dare stand before me—not just admitting, but *boasting* that you are the one who has tormented us all this time. Stealing the necklace I gave her, making people believe her ghost lingered— tearing our wounds open, day after day—"

"If you truly loved her," Neconnu rasps with difficulty, fighting against the wind, "you would tear those wounds open yourself. I am the only one here who cares! I am the only one who will do whatever it takes to bring her back! And I will not let you stop me!"

The other Masters see what Opal is blind to. Her rage is exactly what Neconnu needs: the final insult, the proof—to his mind—

that even Voland's own grandmother did not love her as much as he.

Tears slip from the corners of his eyes. The force of the conjured wind flings them into the distance, and Neconnu is not magus enough to free himself from Opal's attack…but with a twist of his hand, sheltered behind the headstone, he is able to give his grief the freedom his body lacks.

Drop by drop, his tears fall upon Voland's grave.

This is how the tale ends:

On the last day of her mourning, the first day of spring, the Maiden of Sorrow and Joy arrayed in herself in her bridal clothes and went to the grave one final time, as she had done since his death.

But this time when she wept, her tears called forth the spirit of her lost love. He rose in ghostly form and she clasped him to her breast, and when they kissed, the grave released its grip. He became solid and warm; breath moved in his body, and blood flowed through his veins once more.

This is how the Maiden of Sorrow and Joy conquered death: with a year and a day of grief, and true love's kiss.

The wind dies as the Opal Master staggers, eyes wide and brimming, staring at the ghost of her granddaughter. Her tears fall, unneeded and ineffective, to the earth of the grave below.

Neconnu slumps to the ground, smiling up at Voland. "My love," he whispers, so softly it is almost inaudible.

Her gaze drifts downward and alights on him. Her brow furrows. And she speaks.

"Who are you, that has disturbed my rest for so long?"

He scrambles to his knees, clutching at her spectral robe. "I am Harrik Neconnu."

The name sparks no more recognition than it did in the senior Masters. "I do not know you."

"I left flowers at your window," he breathes, gazing up at her. "I let you use my paper fan one day, when yours tore. You smiled at me once during the ritual dance for purification, you—"

The words continue to pour out of him, an increasing flood, a litany of tiny encounters soon forgotten—but not by him. To Neconnu, they are proof of the bond between him and Voland Eleir, a destiny that brought them together, a love that transcends even death.

He climbs to his feet as he speaks, never tearing his eyes from the woman he has adored from afar. The Masters recoil, but none of them speak: however unorthodox this working may be, to interrupt it is a violation not only of protocol but of common sense.

If Harrik Neconnu can bring Voland back to them, not one among them wishes to stop him.

At last he runs out of words. Her ghost stands there, still unmoved. "All those things are things of life," she says, "and did not matter to me even when I breathed. I do not know you. Return me to my rest."

His mouth knots into an ugly line. "I have suffered a year and a day so that we can be together! I may not have mattered to you in life, but I have torn myself apart since your death to have you by my side—I have *killed* someone for your sake—who else would do that? No one! I am the only one who cares! None of them love you as I do! And I will prove it by bringing you back!"

"You cannot give me life."

"I can," he says, chest heaving. "All I need is one kiss. You owe me that much."

Now, for the first time, she seems to see him clearly. "One kiss."

"Yes."

"One kiss, from my cold lips."

"I will warm them."

"For this kiss you have wept for a year and a day, and kept me from my peace."

"You belong with me," Neconnu says. "One kiss, and you will see."

The ghost of Voland Eleir measures him with her gaze. The air itself seems to hold its breath.

"Very well," she says. "One kiss you seek, and one kiss you shall have."

She takes him in her spectral arms, and joins her mouth to his.

Carnelian says, "I deny the degree."

Alabaster shakes his head thoughtfully. "I am not certain. He did something that has never been done before."

"*Vīs mūtandī* at best," Malachite says. "Raising ghosts has been done before, though not by this method. But he chose to submit himself for *vīs faciendī*, and on that point, I think we can agree he has failed."

The body of Harrik Neconnu lies in a heap at the foot of Voland's grave. It is icy to the touch—as cold as the grave he sought to take her from.

"True love," Agate muses, circling the area. "Not a component anyone has ever worked with before, that I am aware of."

"Nor have they done so now," Jade says. He straightens his sleek green robes with a careful hand. "But we have established that obsession is not an effective component for this effect. That is more than we knew before—and I have never heard of a ghost killing in such fashion. Was it because of Voland's talent in life, or Neconnu's working, or the murder he committed, or some other cause? We have both new information and new questions, thanks to this day."

Jasper nods. "And perhaps in the future someone will pursue this line of inquiry, to better result."

Chrysoprase turns away, looking up the slope to where the Opal Master has drawn apart. She is upright, stone-faced, showing neither grief nor vindictive satisfaction. She is simply alone, as she was before.

"Someday long in the future, perhaps," Chrysoprase murmurs. "There is no one left now who shows such promise."

What Still Abides

Let me tell a tale of my father's kin, for in me runs their blood, and so to me falls this burden: to keep the knowledge, the old-thought, the shape of how it began, as my father gave it to me.

Harvest-time it was, the time of reaping and of dying, when his breath stopped and his blood stilled, and they laid his body in the ground. He had a name then, that now is gone; my father knew it but told me not, saying it died with his life, and to speak it now would blight the speaker's tongue.

He died at harvest and they laid him in the ground, axe at his side and barrow built over his head. After that came winter, wolf-cold and sharp. It was a time of hunger, of bellies clenching hard and even kin looking upon one another with an unkind eye. Men tholed ill luck in those long nights: sickness and wound, horses lame and kine lost. Then came spring with storms, grimful rains to drown the fields, and the ground that was his grave became black with mud.

One night a man, Leofnoth by name, son of Leofmaer, hied to the eorl's hall to drink among the thanes, as was his wont, and a shame unto his wife. But when he came there, they saw he was white as bone with fear and his hands shook like leaves in the wind, though he had not yet taken ale. When they asked what had frighted him so, he said he had seen a man standing upon the grave.

For this they laughed at him, and gave him a cup to drink. But rest Leofnoth would not, holding that he told only truth, and furthermore that the man was no thing of this world. And so in the teeth of a storm, three men rode out to see what of what he spake.

Stood a dréag upon the brow of his barrow, feet mud-deep, neither shifting nor breathing.

Warriors they were, bold thanes of the eorl, who had seen that man buried and would swear their oath that he was dead. Yet there stood the lich: frost-shrunken his limbs and grey as old snow, like a curse upon the ground. Bold might they be, but near him none would go, for fear of this unearthly thing. Instead they settled that they would fetch a god-man, whose holy words would lay the wight once more.

But when came the god-man with them to the barrow at the mist-shrouded break of day, cast down he could not what had risen from that earth, for the thing was mightier than he. Whatever words said he, the bone-home neither shifted nor breathed, nor gave any show it saw the thanes and the god-man. Dead had he been, and so was he still, even upon the height of the barrow instead of in its heart.

The first of the thanes set himself to undertake what the god-man could not do, and bring low this weird thing. Fastened he his feet upon the ground, and put the heels of his hands upon the body, throwing against it all his weight. So might he have struggled against the mightiest tree, what little harvest had he for his work. Sought then the next of his fellows, and then the third, and then the three together, but all their strength could not shift the life-left flesh so much as the span of a hair.

Unrestful were their hearts at this, but hid they their fear with laughter, saying that the wight wanted only the freshness of the wind.

And so they left him there, for they could do naught. Came the children of the town to scorn at the thing, daring one another to feel the dréag's dead hand, and their mothers pulled them away.

Seven days after, came there a rider upon a horse, an errand-man for the eorl. As it went by the barrow his horse bolted in fear, dashing up the slope and hurling its burden to the ground. But struck the horse's hoof against the head of the man, and came thus his blood, soaking the loam at the lich's feet.

When came the thanes to gather up the errand-man's body, the dréag was not as he had been. Thick now were the arms withered by winter, ripe as the beginning of rot. But not like life was this; sick-swollen was he, full with the foulness of those who dwell with worms.

Among them were none with will enough to strike the wight. Frightened, left they the errand-man where he lay and rode back to their hall.

Then went out word from the eorl, that he would give rich gold to the man who rid him of this wicked thing. To this call came Aescwulf of the east, a warrior bold whose deeds men heard in tale and song, and said he that his sword would cut down what the god-man's words could not.

Therefore went Aescwulf to the top of the barrow with his sword in his hand, to meet the risen wight. Dry was his mouth and cold his blood at seeing dead flesh stand, but held he to his meaning and his end, lest he shame himself and his good name lose in the eyes of his fellow men.

With keen edge he cut, striking at the sticks of the wight, and meat and bone gave way before his blade. But fell too the sword from Aescwulf's hand: stopped had his heart at the start of his strike, and now he lay dead beside the dréag.

For Aescwulf was great mourning and great thanks, that he had freed the folk from their fear. To his kin gave the eorl the plighted gold and meed besides, for the loss of their fellow in so worthy a work. The wight his men graved in the ground once more, and gave yield to the gods that he should not leave another time.

But when waned the moon, stood the shape again on the height of the hill, the dréag as he had been.

Darker then were the days, grey the sky with clouds, and colder waxed the wind even as the summer grew. Came again the god-man, and four strong men with him, weaponed with whitethorn. For then was it the month of three milkings, and with the wood of that month might they steal the strength that fed his soul. At the god-man's rede bound they the bone-home and broke it from the earth, and once more laid it down where it should keep.

But in this doing, pricked the thorns of the wood into the men's hands, so that their blood fell onto the skin of the wight. Drank the grey flesh these drops and thereafter grew white, shining lich-sick as they steeked the barrow shut.

Still darker dimmed the sun, so that churl and thane and eorl alike dwelt in grave-gloom. Came then the rain almost without halt, drowning the home of seeds, killing the year before it lived. Empty were the keeps of corn after winter's end; hunger was man's dish, and want his drink, and the wolf of death came for many.

Thin grew the sky-sickle and withered into black, and when darkest came the night, rose again the dréag to stand upon the ground.

More gold gave the eorl, and clubs of the crabapple tree, for the boldest men to bear. Now this is the soul-strength of apple: that it is the tree of life, whose wood is bane to things of death. Hewn was this wood from a holy tree, and marked with runes by the god-man, to give it might against the dréag.

Rode forth six men who climbed the hill, and with reckless hearts put themselves against this threat. Scathed their clubs the skin, and with the first blow came the breath of the wolf, the wind of winter, from the wounds they made. Twice struck their arms, and crumbled the blossoms of the hedges into dust. At the last blow, fell the birds from the trees, their feathers breaking against the ground.

From the skin of the dréag wept tears of black blood, that froze the hands of the men. Numb-fingered, took they the raven's food and thrust it into the ground, stopping the way with stone. Then came the women and children, half-starved and scared, with shale from their houses and flint from their fields, to roof over the barrow so naught might grow upon it again. But beneath the blood, the hands of the men were white as midwinter snow.

Long then were the nights, though summer should have made

sweet the sky. Brought the day little sun and no hope, and dwindled horse and kine for lack of grass. All kept watch for the waning of the moon, and what they knew it must bring.

When saw the watchers the wight again, it was the death of hope. No strength of sinew nor holiness of heart could drive the dréag down whither it should be, and its foulness drained the life from the land. Dim were the days and dead the fields, and the men with white hands walked about with empty eyes, stopping neither for food nor for sleep. Dread they woke in those who saw them, and in fear some sought to fight them; but when their foes their hands met, numb went their limbs, as if winter's cold bent their bones. And so left they such men to wander, and those who had not forsaken hope kept far from their path.

But unaware the eorl was not, and had readied himself for this rising.

On the ground before his hall stood a stone. Into this carved the god-man his strongest runes, and wrote over them with his blood, begging the gods, the great ones of the other worlds, to make the stone the stopping of this bane.

Sent the eorl the last of his thanes to the bone-home's bed, where the wight stood again. Dragged they the dréag thence, the white-handed ones walking after, as if they were the thanes of that thing. But stopped they at the stakes that marked the ground of the eorl's hall.

On that ground one woman came forth, having kissed her kin and bid them farewell; Saehild was her name, and well she knew this work would be her death or worse. But for the well-being of her folk, put she her hands to the lich's flesh, cutting it loose with an iron knife. Ulfcytel, best of the thanes, took the body-sticks she bared and laid them upon the stone, that the god-man had named the grinder of the grave. With other stones he broke them, stones carved also with the runes and blood of the god-man, while put Saehild the flesh into a churn of oak, whose staff then beat it soft. White grew their skin where it met bone and meat, but their word they had given, and break it they would not before they were done.

When ended their work, stood they with the empty-eyed ones; but their word they had kept, and so the eorl gave wergeld to their kin.

What abided still they put into a box, whose lid they nailed down with iron. At ene fell dead the god-man, and his body rotted where it lay. At this ill foretoken, more gave in to fear, but said the eorl that all his strength had gone into the spell, and his death was a mark of its might.

Few then yet stood at the eorl's side. Frost-bitten was the wind and dim the light, and held many to their homes; of those who did not, too many walked about bearing white skin and empty eyes. But yet lived hope in the eorl's heart. Took he the box and rode to the wealth-house of the dead, shifting aside the stone to bury his burden where first they had laid the lich, in harvest-time so long before. Then, having roofed the room anew, set he a watch, to see if things would now be well.

The end of this, all men know. Upon the dark of the moon, rose for the last time what men had thought to rid themselves of, fed full by the blood of the god-man, witlessly given. Came then those who yet lived, herded before the white-handed ones, to see the doom of the eorl, torn asunder for seeking to stop this thing. Fell his wound-flood upon the watching ones, waking hunger in their hearts. Crawled they up the barrow's side to beg the blessing from the dréag; cut he his arm, and from it drank they the wolf-wine, which gave to them knowledge of their wyrd, and new ravening.

And so has it been since that day. Never came the sun over this land after that; dwell we therefore in darkness, that men from without hold in fear. From our new god take we our gift, and do his will however he bids. All hail to the holy one, the bestower of blood, the gainsayer of the grave, whose life and might shall be everlasting.

Mad Maudlin

PETER FOUND her slippers just inside his office door. Standard white hospital issue, placed with exquisite care in the small gap between the bookcase and the doorframe, perfectly aligned, heels against the wall.

The police officer just shrugged at Peter's questioning glance. The man was standing a few feet inside the office, thumbs in his belt and elbows tucked against his body, failing to hide his discomfort. He went out quickly when Peter nodded, to take up station in the hall.

Known facts, Peter thought, preparing himself. *Female patient, Jane Doe. Age between thirty and fifty. Unnerving manner.*

Good sense of pitch.

The humming stopped when he drew near, before Peter could identify the tune. He said in a friendly voice, "I found your slippers by the door. Aren't your feet cold, without shoes?"

From beneath his desk came a cockney accent, rough but not hostile. "'Ave to take care of them. Not wear them out. Got a long way to go yet, lovey."

"I see. Where are you headed?" No answer; he hadn't expected one. Peter stepped back to a simpler tactic. "Why are you under my desk?"

He could see her bare feet, through the gap where the modesty panel didn't quite reach the floor. Hard feet, armored with calluses, and profoundly filthy. The nurses hadn't wanted to bathe her. Hadn't wanted to spend any more time with her than necessary. Downtown hospital, veteran staff that had seen absolutely everything three times over, and they didn't want to be in the same room as this woman.

After a long enough pause to establish that the patient wasn't going to answer that question, either, Peter tried a third time. "Is there something I can call you?"

"Been called a lot of things, duck. Mad, Maud, Mad Maudlin."

Maudlin. He couldn't tell if she meant it as an adjective—a play on her name—or a name in its own right, the English variant of Magdalene. Or perhaps she was just playing with sounds. But at least he'd gotten an answer, which was more than the nurses had managed. She mostly just swore at them, called them whores. "May I call you Maud?"

Silence, that somehow carried the quality of a shrug.

"My name is Peter, Maud. I'd like to talk to you. It would be easier if I could see you, though. I don't suppose you might be willing to help? Maybe come sit in a chair, so we can talk?"

Another pause, this one considering. He'd never met someone so able to express herself through a desk. Just as he began pondering his next move, knees dragged against carpet and the feet disappeared. And Maud stood up.

He barely stopped the *Jesus* that wanted to burst from his mouth. Tangled, matted hair, hanging in stringy ropes, its original color impossible to tell. Pointed, thrusting chin, bearing a slash-thin mouth. Strong arch of a nose, and on either side of it, two eyes that could have driven nails into a concrete wall.

Mad Maudlin grinned at him, revealing a disastrous set of teeth. Never taking her eyes off Peter, she rounded the desk, walking on the toes of her filthy feet, and took one of the two chairs.

No wonder the nurses avoid her.

He'd been on the psychiatric ward of this hospital for eleven years, practicing psychology longer than that. He'd seen a lot of homeless people, many of them mentally ill, or implicated in a violent crime. But nobody like this woman.

Peter swallowed, even though he knew she'd spot that sign of weakness. There was no reason to be afraid. The police had taken the weapons she'd carried into the emergency room. Her hands might be skin over tendon and bone, strong as iron, but both the officer and an orderly were just outside, watching through the window in the door; one threatening move—even a hint of a threat—and she would be sedated, bundled into restraints, and dealt with more cautiously. But she hadn't offered violence to anyone.

Not since admission, anyway. The question was whether she'd done so beforehand. And whether Peter could find any hint of where this woman had come from. Mad Maudlin.

He pushed the name away. Delusional behavior, the nurses said; well, he wouldn't help that by calling her "mad." Or overly sentimental, for that matter. Not that she looked sentimental in the least. Peter swallowed again. Not since his first encounter with a violent psychotic had he felt so unsafe in his own office. No, not unsafe—out of control. Whether Maud attacked him or not, the simple act of standing up from beneath his desk had somehow put the reins of this encounter into her hands.

So take them back. "Thank you, Maud," he said. "Would you like some water?"

She nodded. He filled a paper cup from the cooler next to his desk, then pushed it across to her, refusing to let himself retreat in a hurry when that was done. Instead he took the other seat. "If you're hungry, I can get you some food, too."

"Not 'ungry."

She'd come in at seven-fifteen; it was now a little after ten. "Did you have breakfast, Maud?" A wobble of her head, that looked affirmative. "What did you eat?"

"Souls."

He'd expected that. Not the specific answer, but something in that vein; the transfer orders from the emergency room cited her incoherent and frightening speech. *Schizophrenia likely.* "Where was that, Maud?"

Again she displayed those appalling teeth. They lay at all angles in her gums, and some had broken off. If they hurt, she gave no sign. In a dreadful accent he thought was supposed to be southern, she said, "The Good Lord don't keep his kitchens in the attic."

Hell, then. *Delusions show a religious sensibility*, Peter noted. Then underlined it mentally when Maud went on, "Down by the fires, and a big cauldron over them, with all the whores inside. But fire don't bother me. I drank a toast of them, the boiled bitches." She spat on the carpet. "Don't like whores. They wants my Tom, and shan't get 'im."

The name caught Peter's ear. "Who is Tom?"

Maud's attention was on the cup in her hand. "Shouldn't drink this," she mused, holding it up so the morning sunlight glowed through the thin paper. "I'm quarrelsome when I'm drunk. Salt water does that to me, salt and gall, bitter, bitter. Like betrayal."

"I'd like to hear about Tom," Peter said, wondering if this was a clue. The clothes on her when she stumbled into the ER had *someone's* blood on them—a prostitute's? Or Tom's? No alcohol in her system, but she said she was quarrelsome, and if she believed herself drunk it could be almost as bad as the real thing.

She frowned and twisted a quarter-turn away, presenting her right shoulder. "Not much good to be sorry for it now. 'Ow long 'as it been? Ten thousand years? Or ten thousand miles. I confuse the two, I know it. Come such a long way, and 'ave so much farther to go."

"Can we talk about Tom, Maud?"

Paper crumpled in her grip, the remaining water sloshing out to soak the carpet. Droplets fell from her trembling fist, and her gaze struck Peter like a spear, freezing the cry in his throat. For a few breathless beats, he thought she would attack him.

Then Maud's lips twisted in pain, and she looked away.

When he could breathe again, Peter thought, *Paranoid schizo-phrenia.* He relaxed his stiff hands, signaled "all's well" to the orderly watching through the window, and said, "Maud, I'm not sure how much you understand of what's happened, so let me explain a few things. You came into the emergency room this morning, hallucinating and covered in blood. We're concerned that someone may have been hurt, and that you might be able to tell us who." Even if Maud confessed to a crime, he couldn't share that with the police, unless she gave him permission—not likely. But she might let him point them at the victim. Or at least give him something that could lead him to her family, or someone else who knew her. "In return, I'd like to help *you*. I'm a doctor, you see."

With a bitter laugh, Maud dropped the ruined cup and held her wrists out to Peter, still not looking at him. "Chains and whips. I knows the song. You'll cage me and starve me, three times fifteen years, but I'll not die before Doomsday."

His heart gave an unpleasant jolt. *Prior hospitalizations?* Entirely possible; schizophrenics often cycled in and out of treatment. There was no curing them, only drugging them into a semblance of normalcy. And that left them very vulnerable to abuse. Had she been mistreated at another facility, or was this simply more paranoid delusion? "No one's going to hurt you," Peter promised. "There are medicines that doctors sometimes use, in cases like this—do you know if anyone has ever given you olanzapine? Or aripiprazole?" No answer. Maybe the hypothetical other doctors had discovered what the ER had, that none of the usual anti-psychotics made a dent in this woman's behavior. "I'd like to help you, but that's hard when I don't know your medical history. I'm hoping we can just talk. You can tell me what you know, however much you like. Does that sound okay?"

One eye appeared, staring at him through the ragged curtain of her hair. Then the hair moved, and Peter realized it was a nod. He added, "We don't have to talk about anything you don't want to."

Maud still hunched sideways in the chair, curled around herself, weight on her left hip. Not encouraging. He searched for a question specific enough to be useful, neutral enough not to upset her. "I noticed your accent sounds like it's from London, Maud. Do you remember when you came to the States? It must have been a long trip."

Maud scoffed at him. Still behind the concealing hair, but her posture relaxed, feet touching the carpet once more. "Long? That's nothing. I can do it in my sleep. Fifteen thousand miles in a night, one time, guided by the sun." She paused to consider her math, counting on her fingers. "Ten thousand, fifteen thousand—but if it takes only a night walking, then does it count as so much?"

"I would say it does," Peter said. "An airplane goes fast, but it still goes the whole distance. Did you fly here, Maud? Do you remember when that was?" If he could just get one solid detail, he might be able to figure out who she was, and from there have a better idea of what she'd been doing. The police had fingerprinted her while she was strapped to a bed in the ER, screaming profane rhymes at the nurses. But if that had turned up any results, no one had told Peter yet.

He shouldn't have let speculation distract him. He almost missed her hesitant answer. "A long time ago," she whispered, staring vacantly past the arm of Peter's chair. "I used to say the conquest, but I don't remember no more which one it was. People keep conquering places. Wars. The stars fight each other, but them's afraid of me. And the moon...."

"The stars are afraid of the moon?"

She looked at Peter again, but this time the threat in her eyes wasn't for him. "Of me," she said, in a low, animal growl. "I'll murder the bastard. Shake 'is dog till 'e howls, and the dragon and the crow will sing victory instead of dirges. I done it before."

The reference to murder chilled Peter. "You've killed some-one?"

"Drank 'is wine at St. Pancras." She grinned, curving one hand as if it held something—a glass, maybe. "Claret, I think. Or 'ippocras? After I 'ad Tom back."

Tom again. "How did you lose him?"

Maud got up, restlessly, pacing as if she were trapped in the cage she'd spoken of. "It 'appens every time. Over and over again. I don't know 'ow old I am. Last time 'e woke me up—stripped off me clothes—my red-cheeked lad. I 'asn't slept since then."

She halted mid-pace, feet planted apart like an Egyptian statue, shoulders hunched. "Maud," Peter said quietly, knowing it was a risk, "there was blood on your clothes when you came in. Not yours. Who did that come from? The moon? Or Tom?"

The ropes of hair swung, rhythmically, as she shook her head.

"What about the knife in your bag? And your staff? What were those for?"

The laugh was more of a *kack-kack-kack* sound. "Giants. Wouldn't think it to look at me, but I cracks them over the 'ead and they falls. The knife ain't for them, though. 'Ad to feed the fairies. Needed their 'elp. To take me when it's time."

"Feed them what?" Peter asked, not wanting the answer. Or rather, wanting it to have changed, from when the nurses asked.

"Mince pies," Maud said. "They likes children, the fairies do."

The faint smile on her face made him wish he'd never asked. It had happened to him once before, that a patient confessed to a crime; the ethical burden of silence had nearly driven Peter to despair. He still didn't know what had become of that man. But the images still haunted Peter's dreams, and now they would be joined by the bodies of children.

If there *were* bodies. Sometimes schizophrenics did violent things, obeying their delusions. Sometimes they just imagined they did them. Either way, it didn't change Peter's duty: he was a doctor, and he had to help Maud.

Most psychiatrists would pump her full of anti-psychotics and stop there. Even if they found a drug that would work on her, though…Maud appeared to be homeless, and certainly lacked health insurance. Soon she'd run out, or forget to take the medication in the first place, and without any family to help her she'd cycle right back down into illness. *It happens every time,* she'd said. It would happen again. Peter had seen it before.

Unless she really had committed a crime, and they convicted her of it. Then they'd fill her with enough sedatives to put her down for a decade, and leave her to rot.

At least she would stay here tonight. The hospital could manage that much, even for patients like her. It wasn't enough time, but it was all he could give her.

She was staring at him again, pale unblinking eyes. Their desperation cut him like a knife, when his mind was already full of thoughts about how the system was going to fail her. And then her words took him by surprise.

"You don't 'ave to be afraid of me," she said. Her voice held a softness, a resonance, that hadn't been there before, turning the roughness into something much gentler. "All I wants is to find my Tom."

It wasn't the tone of a mother. The possibility that Tom was her son had crossed Peter's mind, but this sounded more like a woman speaking of her lover. "The more you tell me about him," Peter said, "the more I can do to help you find him."

Maud shook her head, lips pressing together so hard they disappeared, leaving her mouth only a slash in her face. Tears lined her eyes, refusing to fall. "I don't remember," she whispered, the admission agonized. "My wits all went when 'e did."

That statement stayed in Peter's mind, caught like a fishhook, long after Maud was taken to her own locked room and Peter went on to other patients.

Microwaving his dinner that night, he played the recording of their session and let the fishhook pull him where it would. Stress could trigger schizophrenic episodes. Perhaps Tom had left her; perhaps more than once, a cycle of stability and disruption that was both cause and effect of her illness. He'd asked one of the nurses to call other psychiatric hospitals, asking if they'd ever had a patient fitting her description.

He realized he was humming that tune, the one she'd been crooning to herself when he came in, and again when they took her away. Peter grimaced and made himself stop. Tomorrow they'd have a list of missing persons in the area: children, men by the name of Tom, anyone who might be the source of that blood. The police were pushing for a fast analysis from the lab, but that could still take weeks; all they knew right now was that it hadn't come from Mad Maudlin. He shouldn't think of her by that name, he knew, but—

The "but" hung suspended in his mind, like the coyote in the cartoons. Just after he realizes the ground is gone, just before he falls.

Peter whispered, "Mad Maudlin." And the tune, the one she'd been humming, resolved itself in his mind. Into one of the English folksongs his mother had loved so much.

The microwave pinged and went dark. Staring at its glossy surface, Peter sang,

"For to see mad Tom o' Bedlam
Ten thousand miles I've traveled
Mad Maudlin goes on dirty toes
For to save her shoes from gravel."

Bedlam. Bethlehem, the old lunatic asylum in London. And Magdalene societies—Maudlin—for degenerate women. Archetypal figures of lunacy…but "Tom" was so common a name, and Peter so determined to avoid thinking of his patient as "Mad Maudlin," he'd missed the connection. Whether his patient's name really was Maud or not, clearly she identified with the figure in the song.

Peter turned with sudden energy toward his CD collection, but stopped with a frustrated noise. Those songs had all been on LP; if they were anywhere now, it was in his sister's basement. But there was the Internet, and a quick search produced a variety of lyrics, Youtube videos of Steeleye Span, Heather Alexander, more. Peter scribbled notes furiously, watched one video after another, scribbled some more. *Mince pies—the man in the moon—Satan's kitchen—*

Tom o' Bedlam. *I now repent that ever / Poor Tom was so disdained,* one version of the lyrics went. *My wits are lost since him I crossed / Which makes me thus go chained.*

He'd assumed Tom was a real person. What if that was just part of the delusion? It might explain why this song, why the identification with Mad Maudlin. Hell, it was almost Jungian in shape. Tom o'Bedlam, a male figure—it suggested the animus, the masculine face of her psyche, estranged. Perhaps she'd rejected it for some reason—rape? Or some other trauma at male hands. And in the rejection, she'd broken her sense of self.

It didn't match any of the usual etiologies for schizophrenia. But it could still be Maud's own narrative, her attempt to craft her disorganized thinking into a coherent shape. And maybe he could use it to help her. She wanted to find Tom; well, if Peter was right, then Tom was within *her*. If Maud could be brought to see that....

Peter glanced at the microwave, saw it blinking "FOOD IS READY" at him. He opened and shut the door to get the clock back. 10:14 p.m. "*I slept not since the conquest,*" he mumbled, thinking. Everyone had to sleep sometimes, but—

Leaving his dinner cooling in the microwave, Peter grabbed a few things and headed for the door.

The nurse glanced at the security monitors and shook his head, blowing out a quick breath of laughter. "No, you won't wake her. She's been pacing all night. Hasn't slept a wink."

"Hang on a moment." The new police officer dropped his feet from the desk and stood up, hooking one thumb through his belt. "This woman might be involved in a crime. And you want to take her for a walk? In the middle of the night?"

Peter faced him without flinching. "Yes, I do. And unless you're ready to charge her with something and cart her off to jail, I don't think you get to give me orders about how I deal with my patient."

"Do you *want* to get killed?" the cop demanded—as if they'd left Maud anything resembling a weapon. "You've heard how she talks. Show a little common sense."

"How she talks and how she acts aren't the same thing. And *common sense* tells me to get her out of these surroundings. She's almost certainly been hospitalized before, so this place is a source of anxiety for her. It might help to talk to her elsewhere."

The cop barked a laugh. "Elsewhere! Nice of you to help the investigation. After we find your body in an alley, we'll know who to arrest for it."

Peter rolled his eyes in annoyance. "Where did you think I was taking her, McDonald's? We'll go to the rooftop garden. Only one door, and if you're afraid she'll escape by leaping off a twelve-story building, I'm sure the fences will stop her. Is that safe enough for you?"

The officer scowled. "I'll come along. Just to be sure."

If Peter had believed the officer's aim was to protect him, he might have been more sympathetic. But the man was more likely to eavesdrop, then claim what he overheard wasn't protected by doctor-client privilege. "You'll wait by the door, out of earshot," Peter said. "And if you argue, I'll leave you here."

The cop accepted it with bad grace. The nurse buzzed the door open for them. The clang of its shutting echoed through the dark, empty hallways; when that faded, Peter could hear the footsteps of an orderly making his rounds, the faint whimpering of a patient somewhere nearby. Yes, it would be better to get Maud out of here, even if it was only for a little while.

But she resisted, when he told her where they were going. "She'll see me," Maud hissed, trying to twist free of his hand.

"Who? Who will see you?"

"The moon!" She glared upward as if she could see through all the intervening floors.

Eleven years working at a downtown hospital carved the lunar calendar into a man's memory; full moons did indeed bring out the crazies. "It's the new moon, Maud. It isn't in the sky right now. You don't have anything to worry about."

Her arm stilled beneath his hand, then relaxed. This time when she pulled free, Peter let her, and she bent to take off her slippers again. With those in hand, she sailed down the hall as if she were a queen processing to court.

They went up the stairs to the garden, and the cop stayed by the door, at Peter's insistence. The night air was warm and dry, the sound of traffic muted by distance and the late hour. Peter led Maud to a bench among the scrawny bushes, about halfway between the door and the roof's fence-girded edge. Once they were seated, he pulled his mp3 player out of his pocket. "I have something I'd like you to listen to, Maud. A song. I think it might be familiar to you."

She took the earphones from his hand, stared at them in confusion. Peter helped her tuck the buds into place. Then he hit play, and the faint, tinny sound of music graced the quiet air.

"For to see mad Tom o'Bedlam / Ten thousand miles I've traveled...."

She sat unmoving through the whole song, ropy hair hiding her face. Peter watched her hand instead, wrapped around the slippers. The knuckles tightened twice, but he couldn't hear well enough to know what lines sparked the reaction. He'd chosen the longest version he could find. Even at that, not everything she'd said was in it; Maud's statements echoed verses Peter had only seen in obscure versions, recorded in eighteenth-century books. Either she'd done the same research he had, or she'd grown up in a household where those versions were sung.

When it ended, he let the silence stretch out for a little while, before prompting her quietly. "Maud?"

Her broken nails dug into the slippers. *"By a knight of ghosts and shadows,"* she sang in an undertone, *"I summoned am to tourney."* She turned slightly to regard Peter, and her eyes gleamed bright through the hair.

"Have you heard this song before?"

"They been singing it for centuries, duck." Maud yanked on the cord until the earbuds popped free, dangling from her fingers. "Add new verses every time I go 'round."

"So the song describes what you feel?"

She laughed at him. "What I've *done.* I remembers enough to know that. It's almost time." Maud tilted her head back, hair falling away, and her profile was hard against the city glow behind.

"Time for what?"

Her teeth bared in a snarl that seemed equal parts eagerness and fear. "For tourney, love. Time to fight. Time to find Tom, and lose him, over and over. Because it don't end; it just keeps 'appening, again and again."

"It *can* end," Peter said. He struggled to keep his voice soothing, not to let his sudden intense excitement break through. "That's what I'm here for, Maud. You're the only one who can make that happen, put an end to the cycle—but you don't have to do it alone."

She sat perfectly still, slippers forgotten in her hand. Then she turned her head, and her gaze struck him with all the force of that first encounter, when she stood up from beneath his desk. "You'll 'elp me?" she asked, and it carried a tiny note of vulnerable hope.

"I'll help you," Peter promised, and on impulse, he reached out to take her hand.

Maud seized his fingers in a grip that almost frightened him into shouting for the cop. Grinning, she bent to put on her slippers, then stood—drawing Peter with her—and spread her arms. "Come on, then," she said, and she wasn't addressing him. "Come, all my soldiers; come to war. It's time!"

She started walking as she spoke, away from the door, toward the edge of the roof. The fence there would stop her leaping, but Peter lagged regardless, uneasy at her sudden aura of purpose. "Maud—"

The wind had picked up. All the hairs along Peter's arms rose, as if there was something, some *things*, racing past him in swirling flocks. As if they were curling around Maud, coming to her call. She was laughing, and the analytical part of Peter's brain, the part that had spent half the night matching her words to verses of the song, found a description of the moment that was all too apt.

With a host of furious fancies—whereof I am commander—

Fancies. Mad imaginings. As if all the delusions of all the patients below them had suddenly swarmed to this place, taking not-quite-corporeal form.

With a burning spear—

She reached out with her free hand, and when it came back, it glowed with a shaft of impossible light.

And a horse of air—

Maud leapt. Dragging Peter up, up, over the fence, an impossible leap, into the sky and *through*—

To the wilderness I wander.

෯෯

He thought he screamed, in that moment between—but they landed hard enough to knock all the air from his lungs and put a stop to sound.

It wasn't the street below, or any part of the city. Not for an instant did Peter expect it would be. There was an *otherness* to this place, going beyond the impossible green of the grass beneath his feet, the cool dampness of the air, the perfect silence devoid of birds or insects or even the wind. But it still gave him a jolt as bad as the landing when he looked up and saw where Maud had brought him.

The field was groomed into a perfect chessboard of grass, bare to the starry sky. Peter and Maud stood on one side, and on the other, a figure sat beneath a canopy, like a king or queen on a throne.

That figure shone with soft, silver radiance. The light emanated from skin, hair, clothing, as if the figure were the full moon in human form. Peter's mind rebelled against the thought, and he jerked his eyes away—only to see the figure wasn't alone. Others stood ranged behind the canopy, creatures twisted like anger and fear and jealousy, creatures that weren't human.

His own side was no better. When he turned to Maud, hoping irrationally that *she* might have an explanation, he saw her own company milling about: *the host of furious fancies*, he thought, that he'd felt on the rooftop. Fairies. They had brought Maud here.

Brought them both. Because Peter had promised.

Maud was staring at him, eyes wide, hand clenched on that spear of flaring light. It wasn't the nail-hard glare of before; she seemed lost and hopeful. Waiting for him to do something.

To help.

"What now?" she whispered.

What the hell could *he* do? This wasn't psychiatry, not any more. One look around told him that much, beyond any possibility of denial. Maud's delusions were *real*. A childhood of listening to folksongs had not prepared him for this.

And yet, he had promised. He couldn't go back on that, even if this was no place for a doctor. It would destroy the trust Maud had given him.

Everything seemed to be waiting, on both sides of the field, for someone to make the first move. Maud, or him. What would happen if they did not act?

Like iron to a magnet, his gaze was drawn back across to the shining figure. And now he saw what he had missed before: two others, standing a step back to either side. On the shining figure's right, an armored form, and on the left, an indistinct male shape, both hidden in shadow.

He'd been more right than he knew, when he dragged up those terms from his half-forgotten undergraduate psychology classes. Animus, anima, shadow, all the complexes and archetypes of Jungian psychology—but the folksong, too, the knight of ghosts and shadows. That would be the armored one; the other....

Tom o' Bedlam.

Peter's breath caught, as if he'd found himself suddenly on the edge of a great fall. Working through it at home, he'd assumed Maud was mad, and used the song as a structuring framework for her delusions. Then he'd come here, and seen that the delusions were real. Now he stood facing what looked a damn sight like the Moon itself, and it was impossible not to think that maybe Maud was right about something else, too. She didn't follow the song—*it* followed *her*.

The logical conclusion, then, was that Maud wasn't schizophrenic at all. But she *was*: Peter knew that, as firmly as he knew his own name. Even though it wrenched his brain, trying to hold both contradictory truths at once. If Maud's delusions were real, then she wasn't mad. But she *was* mad—both creator of and created by this world she'd dragged him into. You'd have to be mad yourself, to wrap your brain around that.

Archetypal figures of lunacy. Mad Maudlin, and Tom o'Bedlam. The only way for them to exist was to be both at once: insane, and also true.

If *that* was true…then maybe this was the right place for a doctor, after all.

Could he *cure* Maud?

Common sense said, *no*. Schizophrenia couldn't be cured, only managed, and the failure of anti-psychotics to work on Maud suggested that even the latter was easier said than done. But then, maybe he'd been attacking it from the wrong angle. Chemicals weren't the answer to a place like this. Here, he had to play by different rules.

The first rule of dealing with a schizophrenic was: *never buy into their delusions.*

Never encourage them, never participate in the things they imagined. But he didn't have much choice. He stood ten leagues beyond the wide world's end, and the only way out was through.

Ignoring the shudder that ran down his back, Peter studied the other side of the field, and tried to bring everything he knew of psychology to bear. Figures of emotion, many of them negative. The Moon, with Tom, the estranged animus, standing in its shadow. *Repressed,* Peter thought. *Disowned. Sent from the self into the shadow, which gives the Moon—mental illness—power over them both.* But how to get him back?

"You told me this has happened before," Peter said. He heard his own voice almost like a stranger's, the level, soothing tones of a psychiatrist so incongruous in this alien field. "You've won Tom back, in the past?"

Maud nodded. "But it's different every time."

Unsurprising. If the solution stayed the same, this wouldn't be much of a struggle. "What did you do, those other times? How did you reclaim him?"

He suspected he knew the answer, from old verses of the song, ones that had fallen out of use. Maud confirmed it. "Jousted against the Whore of Babel once," she said, and something like the old contempt curled her lip briefly. "Tossed 'er on 'er arse— that were a good night. Fought a dragon once. Other monsters, too."

"So you do battle for him?"

"Not always," Maud said, though her brow furrowed slightly. "Sometimes it's other things."

"When we talked before, you said you wanted to kill the Moon.

Do you think that's what you need to do?"

Maud trembled, shrinking in on herself. Peter thought she cast a swift glance across the field. On the far side, the Moon sat serene, as if waiting for Maud to take action. Some verses spoke of it as female, others as male; the actual figure could be either, shifting every time Peter looked.

"Maud," he repeated, softly, "do you want to fight?"

She shook her head, making the ends of the ropes whip back and forth. "Can't."

"Why can't you fight?"

Another brief flicker of a glance, this one more definite. Peter would have bet his hope of going home that she looked at Tom. Shifting the angle of his questions slightly, he asked, "Why do you think fighting brings Tom back?"

The fairies were hovering avidly around them, making his skin crawl. They *were* the delusions of his patients; his, and many others. Perhaps all the patients in the world. In the distance he heard a cruel laugh, and wondered which of the Moon's creatures it was. Anger? Fear? "When you beats someone," Maud said, "you can make them do what you wants."

"But you said you fought a dragon, and other things—not the Moon. And it wasn't always about fighting." He waited to see if she would respond to that, and when she didn't, he went back to Tom. "You disdained Tom, right, Maud? The song says you did— that you somehow crossed him. He's angry at you, and you at him. Why would he come back to you, just because you fought?"

Still no answer. He wanted to just say, *you have to reclaim the parts of yourself you think of as masculine.* But he couldn't just feed her the answer, straight out. That didn't work on ordinary problems, like anxiety or depression; he could hardly expect it to work on archetypal schizophrenia.

He was doing this all wrong anyway—approaching it like a therapist, not like the metaphor of a therapist. With an ordinary patient, talk therapy could take weeks, months, circling around the ideas again and again until the subject was finally ready to admit the truth to herself. That was usually what it boiled down to, the therapist as—

His breath caught a second time. *Oh, hell.* First Jungian metaphors, and now Rogerian psychotherapy? None of this was standard operating procedure for schizophrenia. But his instincts had led him right so far; in the absence of anything better, he might as well keep going.

He bowed to Maud, a reflexive move, inspired by the notion of this place as a tournament field. "Dame Maudlin—"

"I ain't no knight," she said sharply, frowning at him.

Not an auspicious start. "What makes a knight?"

"A knighting." Now her frown suggested he was an idiot.

"A tap of the sword on the shoulder?" Peter asked, in tones that invited doubt. "I would say that by summoning you to this tournament, they have recognized you as a knight—as one worthy to stand on this field of honor." Were those phrases his own, crafted out of childhood memory, or was this place feeding them to him? He wasn't sure he wanted the answer to that question.

Maud wavered. But he needed her to go along with this; without it, none of the rest would make much sense. Grasping at straws, Peter dug in his pocket for a pen, and brandished it in the air. "With this my symbol of authority, I shall make formal what until now has only been recognized in deed. Kneel."

She obeyed, surprising him. Tapping her on the shoulders and head with the pen, he said, "I dub thee Dame Maudlin, champion of all souls lost to madness. For them you shall face your enemy, and emerge victorious. Rise, Dame Maudlin."

She did, with a feral grin. But Peter stopped her before she could charge off. "Would it not be better to observe the formalities? Your victory should not be tainted by misconduct; it would sully your honor as a knight. If you will permit me, then I will serve as your messenger, and request a parlay from the other side."

She objected to this notion almost as much as she had to the title. "Parlay? Thought you said I was 'ere to thrash them."

"All in good time," Peter said, wondering if his idea was wrong after all. But Maud had fought before, and always she found herself back here, having to fight again. Surely it was worth trying something new. "This will give you an opportunity to, ah—" Inspiration struck again. "To deliver your challenge in person."

Maud liked the idea of that. "All right. I'll meet with them. Do I come with you?"

"No," Peter said, hiding his own smile. "I will cross. If they agree, I will wait in the middle of the field, and you and the other party shall come to me."

For all the confidence he projected to Maud, Peter's hackles rose when he stepped out onto the field. The fairies hooted and cheered, a cacophony of sound, echoed from the far side by the howls and jeers of the Moon's creatures. If they rushed him…he didn't think psychological theory was likely to make a very good defense against insanity en masse.

Too late for such considerations now. As soon as he came within range of the Moon, he sank to one knee. "I bring a message from Dame Maudlin."

The silver face was remote, showing only the faintest hint of interest. Peter thought, looking at it, that he could see every lunar symbol he'd ever encountered: tarot cards, werewolves, the Apollo missions, fat smiling faces in children's books, everything superimposed at once upon a single figure. And the voice ran like ice down his spine when the Moon answered. "We are always glad to hear from our subjects."

Should he challenge the implication that Maud was her subject? No, that would come of its own accord, if his idea worked. And if it didn't, well, there was always the brawling option. "Dame Maudlin requests parlay before the tournament begins. With *that* one."

He nodded at Tom o'Bedlam.

The figure stirred within the shadow. This, Peter cautioned himself, was a being as dangerous as Maud; more, perhaps, for Tom was the Moon's captive thrall. Who could say where his loyalties lay?

The Moon sat motionless: not the stillness of a person, whose heart still beat within, but the perfect stasis of something that was never alive at all. Then it said, "Very well, champion of the Sun.

Claim them if you can."

Peter's heart stuttered. Of course the Moon would guess; he could hardly hope to fight for rationalism and sanity here, and *not* have lunacy notice. No, what sent tension dancing along his nerves was the cool amusement in the Moon's voice. It seemed to laugh at something he could not see.

The only way out is through.

Peter retreated to the center of the field and beckoned to Maud, on the far side. As she approached, and the hidden figure stepped out of the Moon's shadow, he closed his eyes, and built a vision in his own mind.

The therapist as mirror, showing the client herself from different angles, all the aspects she lacked the perspective to see—or *would not* see. But the mirror was devoid of judgment; it did not condemn what it reflected. *Unconditional positive regard,* Carl Rogers had called it. That was what Peter must give her now—give *them.* Maud and Tom both.

That was what he must become.

His body flattened into a silver pane, stretching until it blocked all sight from one half of the field to the other. All Maud could see, approaching, was her own reflection, growing larger and more distinct with each step.

A male reflection. Tom o'Bedlam. And on the mirror's other side, Tom himself gazed into Maudlin's eyes.

Both sides feared the other's rejection. Fighting didn't erase that fear. But Peter rejected neither: he understood their madness and accepted it. Through him, they could reconcile at last.

Maud, trembling, reached one hand out, as on the other side Tom did the same.

When their fingers touched, the mirror shattered—and one figure was left standing in the center of the field.

A strong-featured woman, with something of Tom's look about her. He'd been a part of her psyche originally, before repression had driven him into shadow, putting them both under the Moon's control. Together they had passed untold ages, joining and parting, rising briefly toward sanity, only to fall into the depths of madness once more. Always had it been thus.

Always…until now.

The howls of the fairies could have cracked the sky. Whether they rejoiced or rebelled was impossible to tell; it was an elemental cry, thunder following the lightning of the reunification they had just witnessed. The woman raised her hand to them, but it had no effect. A sane person could no longer be their commander.

From his new vantage point, Peter said, "What now?"

The answer came in cool, unruffled tones. "Now she returns to the world of the Sun. She was an ordinary woman once, and so she is again. She has no place here."

The woman was leaving the field, heading to the side, away from both gathered armies. "Will she remember any of this?"

"As a dream, nothing more. Only the mad believe in such things as these."

The mad—and the psychiatrist who healed them. Peter wondered what he was going to say when *he* got back. He would never look at a patient the same way again, now that he'd seen the creatures that personified their syndromes and disorders, and the entity that ruled over them.

And what would the world do, without Mad Maudlin and Tom o'Bedlam to embody its madness?

Peter turned and bowed to the Moon. "Thank you. You have opened my eyes in a way I never imagined possible. I will carry the effects of it with me forever."

The Moon bestowed a serene smile upon him. "Yes. You will."

"There wasn't any evidence of a crime," Peter said, "other than the blood. Which didn't match any known victim, and there wasn't anything to connect her to any missing persons. So in the end, they let her go."

Shawna Cross, one of the hospital's junior doctors, shook her head in amazement. "No, that part makes sense. What I'm sticking on is the bit where you say she made a full recovery."

"As near as I can tell," Peter cautioned. "I haven't seen her in a year. But she certainly wasn't a danger to anyone any more." Peter downed the last of his coffee, then signaled to the waitress for the check.

"And you did it by *talking* to her?" Shawna shook her head. "One conversation in the garden, and she comes back cured. If that's true—and I'm not saying I buy it—then I can't believe you *quit*. I get half a dozen schizophrenics every week, a lot of them repeat customers. Can't do much for them, and it breaks my heart. We could use your magic, man."

Peter smiled, digging for his wallet in his back pocket. "Sorry. But I can't do it anymore; I can't look at those people and see them as diseases to be cured. You have to accept them for who they are."

"Easy for you to say. They aren't vomiting on you anymore, or trying to stab you with their own IV needles." Shawna dropped a few bills on the table. "Speaking of which, my break's over. Back to the salt mines, I guess. Thanks for the story."

Peter whispered his reply to the restaurant door, swinging shorter and shorter arcs in Shawna's wake. "They still do those things. But it's okay. I accept them anyway."

"Naturally you do," the Moon said, sitting where Shawna had been. Its radiance dimmed all the lights in the restaurant, casting everyone into shadow. "You cannot condemn the realm to which you now belong."

The memory of the time when he *would* have condemned it was fading, almost forgotten. The Moon had shown him a hundred thousand variants on madness, more than he ever could have imagined before—and Peter loved them all.

"Come, my champion," the shining figure said. "We have much work to do."

Cruel Sisters

THE HARP IS a gruesome thing. Long bones for the pillar; breast-bone for the board; the curve of a spine for the instrument's neck and knee. At the head sits a skull, grinning eyelessly at all who flinch away.

I saw it when they paraded it through the streets after the revolt, carried on high like a triumphant hero. Even without flesh, I knew that grin.

The story's been told from one end of what used to be our kingdom to the other. The death of the younger princess, supposedly from illness—but one day a minstrel arrived at court, bearing the macabre harp. Its strings, spun from golden hair and tuned by delicate finger-bones, sang out all the crimes and sins of her royal kin, from her murderous elder sister to her treasonous younger brother to her cruel, capricious, contemptible father the king.

Very little of it was a surprise to anybody. But it seems there's nothing like the testimony of a restless ghost to spur people to revolution at last.

And if the voice sounds very little like that of the dead princess…it's a haunted harp. No one questions its authenticity. And I am not about to tell them.

The chapel is grave-quiet as I creep through the shadows toward the harp. It can already see, even though it lacks eyes; I shouldn't be surprised that it can see in the dark. But I still jump when its ethereal voice thrums into the silence.

"Sister."

Dread grips my soul. I suspected, yes—but it is another thing to *know*.

"You lied," I whisper back, my voice as thin and dry as dust. "Why?"

"You mean, why did I condemn them, instead of you."

The jolt thudding up my arms as I shoved her into the water. It was a stupid argument, and my oath to God, I thought she was exaggerating her distress. She loved to swim in the summer months. But it was early spring, and the water snow-cold, and she never went swimming in her dress. Afterward, I told myself it was the dress that killed her, not me, not me.

I can't find the words to reply. She answers her own question anyway. "Because there are things that matter more than you, my dear, treacherous sister. Like the fate of this country. If I could bring down the monarchy by pretending to be the dead princess…it was hardly a choice."

How many of their crimes were real, and how many invented to rile the mob? I can't ask. I don't want to know. We always disagreed on this anyway, and it's too late to convince either of us of anything. The country I loved is gone.

My cold hands seek out the warmth of my pockets, and the reassuring weight within. "But now. Are you going to tell?"

"That you killed me? No. Not yet."

The tension that started to unwind at *no* twists tight again at *not yet*. The golden hair hums with a sound that might be amusement. "Her late highness is so beloved, after all. I can't risk anyone guessing I'm not who I claim to be. Not when there are others to bring down first."

I retreat a step. "Others?"

"Why stop at the royal family? I have a chance to remake this land into what it should be. Sleep without fear, sister mine; if I come for you, it will be many years from now. And perhaps not even then."

The harp may see without eyes, but she cannot see the truth. My fear is not for myself. I came here prepared to defend my life… but the danger I've found is something else entirely.

My sister's strings twang in sudden alarm. "What are you doing?"

"I didn't mean to kill you that day," I say, my voice trembling. "But you should have stayed dead. So I will finish what I started."

Her finger-bones are pegged in place, winding her hair tight. She can speak, she can sing, she can scream—but she cannot stop me as I pull the hammer from my pocket and swing.

The Twa Corbies

IN ALL the fairy stories, when the hero is magically gifted with an understanding of the speech of birds, it actually does him some good. A robin brings him a message from his true love, or a bluebird tells him about buried treasure, or a starling warns him of a traitor among his companions. It doesn't really work that way, though—not in real life. Birds mostly talk about seeds and worms and the breeze and nest-building and the state of their eggs. I should know; I've been listening to them for seven years.

In all that time, they've only ever said one thing that interested me, and that one almost got me killed.

I blame the ravens. Of all the breeds I've been forced to listen to, ravens are my least favorite; bird-talk about seeds may be boring, but bird-talk about carrion is just nasty. Ravens have a tendency to go into all sorts of detail I simply don't want to hear. I avoid them when possible.

But this time I didn't have much choice. I was walking between towns when a pebble managed to work itself into my boot; I tried to ignore it for a little while, but it got really annoying, and at last I had to stop and get rid of it. That, of course, meant finding a place to stop. I'm not exactly fastidious, but the sky had been dumping rain on me for six days, and the road was a sea of mud. I trudged on, the pebble annoying me more with every passing second, until at last I came across a low stone wall. I heaved my pedlar's pack onto the top, then hopped up to sit next to it.

A raven fluttered to a landing in a scrawny ash tree nearby as I unlaced my boot and pulled it off. I ignored the bird; ravens at least have the decency not to chatter to themselves, the way sparrows do. I figured I could work in silence.

But a second bird joined the first a moment later, and they started talking.

"Where shall we feast today?" the second bird asked the first.

I began very hastily to search for the pebble in my boot.

Unfortunately, I have a really hard time tuning birds out. People are easier; don't ask me why. Maybe it has to do with me spending so much time on the road, on account of being a pedlar. At any rate, I found myself an unwilling audience to their conversation.

"I have found a fresh morsel just beyond the dike," the first bird said.

The second raven quorked in interest. "What sort of morsel?"

I intensified my search for the elusive pebble.

"A *human*," the first bird said with relish. "Of the sort that is encased in metal."

My boot almost slipped from my chilled fingers.

The second bird let out an irritated caw. "They are a nuisance to eat. The metal gets in the way."

"Its head is uncovered," the first raven said. "Its eyes are yet there; we may eat them if we hurry. And its hair could be used for nest-material."

Back to nest-building—just like a bird. But that thought was irrelevant to what the rest of my mind was thinking.

Encased in metal.

Only knights wore armor.

The second raven sounded tempted as it said, "Perhaps. Are we likely to be disturbed?"

"I think not," the first bird said. "It is but new-dead. And no one knows it has died."

"Did you see it die?"

The dreadful eagerness in the second raven's voice made me shiver. The first one replied, "I did. It was riding alone, on a horse, and then it fell off and died. It had only a hawk and a hound for company, and none has come near it since then."

The pebble fell at last into my searching fingers, which had gone about their task without the rest of me. I tossed it to the ground, then jammed my boot back onto my foot and began to lace it up quickly. A knight, lying dead in a ditch, and no one knew he had fallen.

I couldn't just leave him there, for these unpleasant birds to peck out his eyes. Granted, if he was a knight in full armor, I had about as much chance of carrying him as these ravens did of carrying me, but at least I could see if he had his shield with him; if I knew his coat of arms, I could tell the people in the next town that he had died. They might reward me for the information.

It crossed my mind that they might instead accuse me of killing him, but I didn't worry about that overmuch. I'm just a pedlar; how could I kill a knight in armor? Besides, the raven had said the man fell dead at no outward attack. His heart had probably given out.

With my boot finally laced, I hopped off the wall on the other side and slung my pack onto my back. I could see the dike the first raven had referred to, just a short way across the field, and began to slog toward it through the ankle-deep mud.

As I went, the two ravens flapped past me.

I did my best to hurry, but the mud sucked at my boots and slowed me down. By the time I crested the top of the dike, the ravens had already landed on the body of what was unmistakably a knight, lying in the filthy water at the bottom of the ditch.

"Here now!" I called out to them, making shooing motions with my hands. "Get away from him! Off! Fly off!"

The smaller raven looked at the larger. I had no idea which was which, from their previous conversation, and they all sound alike to me. "It *does* understand us," it said.

Damned clever ravens. "Yes," I said; this was not the first time I'd had to explain myself to birds. "I was granted a favor a long time ago, and like an idiot, I said I wanted to understand birds. Now buzz off. You can't eat this man."

The larger raven cocked its head at me. "Oh can't we?" And its beak darted down.

"Stop that!" I skidded down the muddy slope toward them, and as I regained my balance I saw an amused gleam in the larger bird's eye. It had not actually taken a bite of the dead man; it was only taunting me.

"Not yet, anyway," I was forced to say. "Please, just have the decency to wait until I'm gone. I don't want to watch you peck off bits of him."

"So go away," the smaller raven suggested rudely.

I would, and gladly, in just a moment. But first I had to figure out who the dead knight was, or at least get enough identifying characteristics that I could describe him to someone.

His eyes were open and staring, glazed over in death; in life they would have been a lively blue. I shuddered away from looking at them for too long. His hair, where it was not muddied and brown, was a rich gold color; he was young, and had probably been quite handsome before he died. Now, however, his pale skin had taken on that ugly pallor that corpses have. I was lucky he hadn't yet started to rot.

But his armor—chain-mail with a little bit of plate—was unremarkable, and he wore no tunic to show me his coat of arms. His shield was nowhere in sight.

"How did he die?" I asked the birds.

The larger raven shifted his feet on the man's shoulder. "You were listening, weren't you?" it asked snidely. "It fell off its horse."

"Just fell? Didn't he clutch at his heart or anything? Sway in the saddle? Look ill?"

The raven quorked to itself for a moment, saying nothing intelligible, then admitted, "Well, yes. It looked like it wasn't doing very well. That's why I followed it. When I first saw it, it was fine, but then it suddenly went very green and dropped its shield and I thought it might be about to die." The bird fluttered its wings proudly. "I was *right*."

Dropped its shield. I'm not much of a tracker; in this muddy trench, I could not make out the hoofprints of a horse. "Where did it come from? Did it drop its—*his* shield near here?" I needed to get away from these damn birds; I was starting to talk like them.

"If I tell you will you go away and let us eat in peace?"

The thought of leaving the dead man here for these ravens

turned my stomach, but there wasn't much I could do to stop them. I had no horse, and the knight's was long gone. "Yes."

"Come on."

The raven took to the air, flapping up over the other embankment. I followed, slipping in the mud, cursing the ill-fortune that had put a pebble into my boot just at the right moment to get me caught up in this mess. Why couldn't it have happened a mile sooner, or later?

Or why couldn't I just have ignored the damn birds and walked on?

A narrow track ran along the embankment on that side. The raven had flown a short distance along it, and now sat on the ground, waiting for me with an impatient air. I hurried to see whether it was telling the truth or not.

It was. The knight's shield lay face-down in a thorny bush, as if it had been dropped from horseback. I dragged it clear and turned it over to find the knight's blazon. Two crossed spears done in white on a black field.

"I know this blazon," I muttered, talking to myself more than to the raven. As I've already said, I don't like having conversations with them. "It's Lord Tergram's." But that couldn't be him in the ditch; Lord Tergram was an older man, with his hair gone grey. The dead knight must be his son, the one who had gone off to war—I couldn't remember his name.

"Can I eat it now?" the raven asked, shifting from foot to foot.

I blanched. Somehow it was much worse to think about the bird eating the dead knight now that I knew who he was.

"You promised," the bird reminded me, and glared at me balefully.

I wanted to say no. But knowing the man was the younger Tergram did not make me any more capable of stopping the bird. I sighed and nodded.

The raven said nothing more, but flew off.

I returned to the road and my journey. Tergram was the overlord of the very town I was headed for. I would return his son's shield to him, and hope someone got to the dead knight before the ravens did too much damage.

The guards at the town gate were huddled inside their little tower, hiding from the rain. Two of them emerged, though, when I came slogging up.

"I need to talk to Lord Tergram," I said.

The fatter of the two guards shook his head. "Lord Tergram's dead."

My heart skipped a beat. "Lord *Rallec* Tergram?"

"He died about a year ago." The guard was plainly not interested in this conversation; he wanted to get back inside where it was dry.

I shared that sentiment. "Then I want to speak to whoever's in charge now."

"And why should her ladyship see you?"

I supposed I did not look like someone who deserved to see her ladyship; I was soaked to the bone and spattered with mud up to my hips, thanks to my little jaunt into the fields. I still had a card to play, though. I held up the shield. "Because of this."

The skinnier guard peered through the rain at the shield. "Whassat?"

My impatience slipped its leash a little. "It's the shield of Lord Rallec's son," I snapped, and only barely swallowed the "idiot" I wanted to stick on at the end.

"Right," the fatter guard said, and for a moment I thought he was expressing disbelief. But when I looked at him, he was nodding wearily. "I'll take you to her ladyship."

As we hurried through the half-flooded streets, it occurred to me to wonder who "her ladyship" was. Not Rallec's wife; I seemed to remember him being a widower. Had he remarried? No, it had to be the son's wife.

Great. I was going to tell a woman that her husband was lying dead in the mud. This day was getting better all the time.

The Tergrams were not a powerful family, for which I was grateful; a grand hall would have put the cap on my discomfort.

Instead I was shown into a room which, while big and impressive and hung with tapestries, was something I could deal with. My escort muttered to another guard, who muttered to a man standing at the other end of the hall, who muttered to the woman seated in a huge carved chair beneath the Tergram banner, while I waited and dripped on the floor.

The man beckoned me forward.

I advanced across the floor, painfully aware of my appearance, and made the best bow I could while holding the shield. "My lady," I began, wondering if there was any good way to break this news. Probably not. "I'm sorry to be the one to tell you this, but your husband's dead."

She did not scream; she did not weep. She didn't even stare. "I'm aware of that, thank you."

I blinked. Aware of it? What the hell?

"We heard months ago," she added calmly.

My familiarity with corpses was limited, but the knight in the ditch had *not* been dead for months. Even the ravens had called him "fresh." And if these people knew he was dead, why hadn't they fetched his body for decent burial?

I must have spoken out loud, at least for that last thought. I usually have the sense not to talk about the birds. The lady looked at me as if I were an idiot. "Because no one could *find* his body," she said.

"*I* found it," I said, and for the first time I had the attention of everyone in the room. I held up the shield in the sudden silence. "I've got this to prove it."

The lady sat quite upright in her seat. "You…found his shield?" she whispered hoarsely. "You've come from the war?"

"No," I said. She was making my confusion worse instead of fixing it.

"Then where did you find that?"

"About an hour's walk south of town," I said. That, at least, was something I was sure of. "He's lying in a ditch out there, and if you don't want ravens eating too much of him, you should send someone for him right away."

"He's *not* in a ditch," she said, her voice harsh. "When his father died, we sent to him, and the messenger came back saying he had been killed in the war."

"Then somebody screwed up," I said, forgetting to be polite. I hadn't expected this sort of trouble when I decided to be a good guy and bring news of the son's death. "Because your husband really is out there. Send someone out to look if you don't believe me."

The lady looked reflexively to the man at her side. He nodded. "My lady, with your leave, I will check the truth of his words."

"Do," the lady said. "And in the meantime, someone get this man cleaned up. He's dripping."

How the raven found me, I couldn't tell you. Maybe there's a conspiracy of birds, and the town pigeons told him. All I know is, I was changing into relatively dry and clean clothes from my pack when he fluttered onto the windowsill.

"This is *your* fault, isn't it," he accused me.

I stared at him. "You again? Why are *you* here?"

"You promised we could eat in peace," the raven said. I thought he was the larger one, the one who had found the body in the first place, but without the other for comparison it was hard to tell. "Now more humans have come and taken our food away."

I supposed that *was* my fault. "Sorry," I said, and did not mean it in the least. "The people here wanted to bury him."

"Well, they did *that* all right," the raven said disconsolately. "Now I won't get to eat its tongue."

I was in the middle of congratulating myself for having saved the young lord from being snacked on by ravens when the actual words registered on me. "They buried him *already*?"

The raven glared at me. "Yes. It's a waste, if you ask me."

I wasn't asking. What *I* wanted to know was, why had they buried him already? That made no sense at all.

At least, it didn't make any sense until they took me back to the hall.

"We found nothing," the man who had led the riders said.

The lady fixed unfriendly eyes on me. "So. You are a liar, as I suspected."

A *liar?* I might be an idiot, for getting involved in this mess in the first place, but never a liar. "I brought you his shield," I reminded her. Surely that was proof.

"Which you stole off the battlefield, or obtained from someone else," she said. "And, for reasons only you can know, you felt the need to come torment me in my grief by telling me vile falsehoods about my poor, late husband." She didn't sound very tormented or grief-stricken; she sounded angry.

That was so far from the truth that I wanted to scream. Instead I gritted my teeth and searched for something that would get me out of this before my day got any worse. "Maybe…maybe I was mistaken, my lady." Mistaken how? I couldn't say they'd searched in the wrong place; I might not know what was going on, but it didn't take a genius to figure out that the riders had hidden the body, and would not produce it no matter what. At this point I didn't care why; I just wanted to stop being involved. "Maybe someone was trying to deceive me, my lady. I did find your husband's shield in the ditch, I swear to that, and there was a man there in armor. Maybe…someone else is trying to torment you, as you say."

Worst lie I've ever put together, but it did the job. If by "did the job" I mean "kept me out of the dungeon."

Okay, so I *do* lie occasionally, but only when there's great need.

The lady glared at me. "You will leave this town," she said. "You will leave and not come back. I do not want to see your face here again."

Fine by me, I thought, and didn't even protest when they sent me back out into the rain.

I was all prepared to put that disaster behind me when the raven found me again.

"Go *away*," I snarled through clenched teeth. "You've caused enough trouble for one day."

Then a hawk came arrowing out of the damp air to land next to the raven on the fence. She looked at the raven, then at me. "Can he really understand me?"

"Oh, *no!*" My protest made both birds flutter their wings. "I am *not* talking to you anymore. Any of you. Leave me alone!"

The hawk fixed me with her bright eyes. Normally I'd rather talk to a hawk than a raven, but not right now. I remembered well enough what the raven had said about the dead knight. If this wasn't Tergram's hawk, I would eat my shoes. And hawks are very single-minded creatures.

"This one tells me you have a care for my master," the hawk said.

"No," I said immediately. "I just wanted to get him buried. That's done, so I'm done." Even if the knight had been dumped in an unmarked grave.

"I would not count on that," the hawk said.

Against my will, she had my attention. "Count on what?"

"Being done."

I had a sinking feeling in the pit of my stomach.

"My master was murdered," the hawk said.

"Now wait a second," I cut in. "This raven here said your master just fell out of his saddle and died. He didn't say anything about an arrow or an attack."

The hawk mantled, and it occurred to me that she could rip me bloody if I made her angry. "He was murdered by magic," she said.

Your average man would have laughed this statement off. Your average man, though, has never caught a pixie skulking around his fire one night, and has never forced that pixie to grant him a wish. I had proof of magic, all right, although I seriously regretted asking to be able to understand birds.

I had thought they might be able to give me directions on the road.

The rain was tapering off to an annoying mist. I stood in the middle of the road and tried to tell myself to keep walking. The knight had been murdered by magic, his hawk said. His lady thought he had died months ago. His lady's right-hand man had hidden the knight's body and then lied to her about it.

This had all the marks of something I should have never gotten involved with in the first place.

But if that man was responsible for murdering the knight, then the lady deserved to know.

Besides which, I had a hawk sitting not far away with a look in her eye that said she was not going to leave the matter alone until I helped her.

I had a vision of myself pecked to a bloody ruin, and snarled.

"All right," I said reluctantly. "Where's he buried?"

The riders had not buried the body very deeply, and the ground was soft. A few minutes of work coated me in mud and revealed the knight's body.

"Now what?" I asked the two birds who were watching from a tree.

"Can I eat him?" the raven asked.

I ignored that. The hawk fluttered down to land on her dead master's chest and nodded her beak toward his hand. "He put that ring on and it made him very ill."

I looked at the ring she had indicated, checking my urge to reach out for it. The ring in question was a heavy signet; with the mud on it I couldn't be sure, but my guess was that it was the Ter-gram seal. "Why didn't he take it off?"

"It wouldn't come off," the hawk said. "He tried."

So he hadn't been entirely stupid. The question was, what should I do now? I had an apparently cursed ring and an obviously dead knight. If I brought them to the town, at least I could prove to the lady that I had been telling the truth—assuming, of course, that the guards let me in. But what proof did I have that he'd been murdered?

I looked around and sighed. The knight had been buried in the lee of another low stone wall, farther from the road. There was a wood right nearby; I could go cut branches from that to make a sledge, and use that to drag the body. The mud might actually help me out, by making it easier to slide things. But what would be even better would be to find a farmer who had a horse I could use. According to the hawk, the knight's own horse was long gone, and so was his hound.

The sun was headed for the horizon; I didn't have a lot of time to waste. I flicked my wet hair out of my eyes and looked at the hawk. "Do me a favor. Fly around here until you find a nearby house, okay? You know what a house is, right?" She glared at me, offended. "When you find the nearest one—preferably in the general direction of the town—then come back here and tell me."

The hawk opened her beak, but I cut her off before she could protest. "If you tell me this is beneath your dignity, I'm going to dump your master back in this hole and forget the entire thing."

The threat worked. She flew off.

I sat down with my back to the wall to wait. At this point I didn't care about the mud; I was just about as dirty as I could get already.

Not much time had passed before I heard hoofbeats squelching across the fields. The hawk must have found someone quicker than I thought, and brought him to me already.

But wait—that thought made no sense at all. Farmers can't understand bird talk. How could the hawk have brought some-one?

I leapt to my feet just as two horses came sailing over the wall and skidded to a halt in the mud.

"Well," the knight's lady said in a cold voice, turning her horse to face me. "It seems you are yet inclined to meddle."

I clenched my teeth and called myself nineteen kinds of idiot. How had I been so stupid? Her calm was not that of a widow who has come to terms with her grief; it was the calm of a murderess who never mourned her husband's passing in the first place.

At her side, the man she had dispatched to hide her husband's body smiled unpleasantly.

The lady looked down on the mud-covered form of her late husband and made an irritated sound. "If only he had done as he should, and died the moment he put on the ring," she said. "Where he got the strength to survive for so long, I do not know." Her cold gaze lifted to regard me. "But it does not matter. He is dead, and I am Lady, and no troublesome pedlar is going to change that."

I stood with my back to the wall, my heart so far up in my throat I could taste it. There was nowhere I could run; they would ride me down.

"My love," the lady, the witch, said to the man at her side. "Do me the favor of killing this man."

"Gladly," the man said, and his expression echoed it. He would enjoy killing me.

I looked desperately about for an escape as he unhooked a crossbow from his saddle.

"Would you like help?" the raven asked me from its perch in the tree.

Neither the lady nor the man reacted. They could not understand him; all they heard was squawking. I could barely speak for terror, but I managed to yelp, "Yes!"

The man was loading a quarrel into the crossbow.

"Can I eat *their* eyes?"

The murdered knight might deserve better, but these two did not. "*Yes!*"

The man lifted the crossbow and aimed it at me.

The raven arrowed down out of the tree and flew directly for his face. The man swore and jerked instinctively away; the quarrel flew, but skipped off the top of the stone wall, missing me by a hair.

The raven flew off, screaming something unintelligible, and left me alone with the two of them.

Some help, I thought bitterly, and ran like hell for the wood.

"Get him!" the lady screeched, and within an instant I heard hoofbeats behind me. I was going to die anyway; the raven had only delayed it for a moment.

Then the birds came.

They poured out of the wood like a flood, thundering past me on a thousand wings. I could not identify half of them; they flew too quickly, and besides, their kind did not matter. What mattered was that they attacked the riders pursuing me, while the raven circled and shrieked battle cries, urging them on to blood.

As I reached the periphery of the wood, I had to turn around. The horses had stopped; their riders were flailing their arms, trying to fend off the birds. They did not stand a chance, though. Here and there they struck a small body, stunning the bird or occasionally hurting it, but there were too many. Their screams rose above those of the raven.

And then the hawk plummeted from the sky like a taloned rock and struck the lady, and she toppled from her horse into the mud. The man followed a moment later, vanquished by a thousand little birds.

He lived, actually—at least for a little while. The lord who came in to clean up the mess afterward sentenced him to death, so he hung in the end, with the wounds still visible on his face where the birds had attacked him. The lady died out there in that field, though; the hawk had seen to that.

The murdered knight was buried properly, where the ravens cannot get at him. The one who got me into all this trouble didn't hold that against me, though; he made quite a feast of the lady's face before anyone arrived to take care of her body.

I might have been a bit slow getting people out there.

I got a bit of a reward for the whole thing; they found evidence in the lady's chambers of her witchcraft. It didn't make up for nearly being shot, though, and it *certainly* doesn't make up for what's happened since.

You see, some of the birds got hurt in that attack, and I couldn't just abandon them, not after they saved my life. So I nursed them back into health while all that trial business was going on, and the upshot of it all is that now the birds *like* me. They follow me wherever I go, and tell me about the worm they caught that morning and the way the breeze is blowing and how they think their eggs might hatch soon.

All except the ravens. *They* all snicker among themselves when they see me, and ask if I'd like to see the dead bodies *they've* found.

Next time I catch a pixie, I know what wish I'm going to make.

Oh, My Cursed Daughter

Oh, my darling daughter. You cannot trust him; you cannot trust them. You cannot *ever* trust them.

You and your friend Oona have always played silly games. Tossing pennies and wishes over the waterfall, praying to the spirits to bring you love. Casting curls of apple peel behind your shoulder, hoping they will form the initial of the man you will someday marry. But those are the games of young girls, and now you are older; now Oona's games have changed.

The blouse you wear to the autumn festival is hers. *You* own nothing that drops so low on your youthful breasts, and mine I burned long years ago. The red staining your cheeks and lips comes from berries the two of you picked together, giggling all the while. The trinket you dangle from your neck, on a long cord so it invites the gaze low—that, too, is Oona's.

The look you wear, along with the blouse and the berry juice and the trinket, is half embarrassment, half defiance. Waiting for me to comment. Shifting to surprise when I do not.

'Tis all embarrassment, through and through, when I find you later with Mihal.

Like you, he has put away the games of children. Now it is dancing; now it is ale in abundance. When I come upon you behind the barn, he lies on the ground, his head pillowed on your shawl. You hold his hand, stroking it as you sing a quiet song, soothing the wretchedness brought by too much drink. You are embarrassed to be caught thus, but not guilty.

Nothing has happened, after all.

Oh, my foolish daughter. You cannot trust him; you cannot trust them. You cannot *ever* trust them.

You know the things they whisper about me. You know why Oona has been your only friend, why only Mihal would approach you at the festival, low-draped blouse or no. This village shuns me, fears me, hates me. Those things are your inheritance as well.

That winter is a hard one, with little snow, but sharp-frosted. More than once you come home to find our front door stained with dung, thrown by some villager who blames me for the cold. For their children who fall ill; for their sheep who die. Sometimes the dung is thrown at *you*. And so you turn more and more to Mihal, sneaking out to meet him when you think I will not notice.

Come spring, when he and some of the other men take the season's shearing to market, you are bereft. Oona has her own man now; they are to be married in early summer, before her belly grows too large to ignore. You envy her, as if she has achieved some great victory. But without her, without Mihal…you have only me.

I cannot control the weather, whatever the villagers think. But I can do this much for you, my child.

You drink the tea I give you, and I finish the rest. Together we bend over my good bowl, the one I never let you touch. The water I pour in splashes, ripples, stills.

And you see.

Mihal in the market town. So many people there—more, far more, than you have seen in your short life. Strange accents and stranger clothes, merchants come from afar. A whole world beyond the life of this village and its fears.

A world of temptation.

You with your berry-stained lips had nothing on the women in town. The matrons dress soberly, but others drag their blouses lower than even Oona, paint themselves from bosom to hair. They laugh coyly at Mihal, trail their fingertips across his chest. They lean in close.

Mihal's eyes flutter…

…and then he turns away.

Your shoulders sag in relief as you release the breath you were holding. Beaming, you fling your arms around my stiff shoulders, and then you hurry out the door to find spring flowers to press dry and give to Mihal when he returns.

Oh, my stubborn daughter. You cannot trust him; you cannot trust them. You cannot *ever* trust them.

It is high summer when the ring vanishes from your hand.

The golden ring I gave you, simple and slim, that for years has graced your hand. The moment I notice its absence, I know what it must mean.

There is no embarrassment this time, only defiance. You hold your back straight, and you tell me that you and Mihal have pledged your troth. He has your ring—*my* ring—upon his smallest finger; his, too large for you to wear, is on a cord about your neck, where once you hung a trinket to draw his eye.

You think this promise between you means something. You believe your love is stronger than anything. Stronger than the villagers' fear. Stronger than me.

Despite all my efforts, I still have not taught you the truth.

On the day Mihal goes to buy a horse, you wait for him along the road outside the village. He takes longer than he ought; it is near twilight when he returns. Ideal timing for an ambush.

You rise out from cover, pistol cocked and raised. The horse rears in surprise, almost throwing Mihal to the ground. The hat on your hair, the kerchief over your face, the trousers you wear—all these disguise you. He thinks you a bandit, and when you demand his purse, he hands it over. When you demand his pocket-watch, he unhooks it from his vest. When you demand the horse, he dismounts and gives you the reins.

Men speak grandly of their courage until it is put to the test. To save his skin, Mihal will surrender anything.

But when you demand the golden ring from his hand…

"Shoot me if you must," he says, his chin high as if to escape the rising waters of fear. "But this ring was given to me by my beloved Sovay, who all her life has had no one but a frivolous friend and a bitter, jealous witch for a mother. If I surrendered this ring, then I would betray her trust—and that, I will never do. I will die first."

You stand, frozen. Your finger is rigid on the pistol's trigger. You might as well be a statue in the lane.

Mihal waits. Then he nods and, with stiff, frightened steps, walks past you to the village.

Oh, my defiant daughter. You cannot trust him; you cannot trust them. You cannot *ever* trust them.

I have played my hand too openly. By the time you return home, you know. There is no use in me denying anything.

Yes, I ensured Mihal's drunkenness the night of the festival. Yes, I arranged for you two to be unchaperoned. Yes, I came when I did because I hoped to catch you in an indiscretion—to show you Mihal loved you only for your breasts and your berry-painted lips.

Yes, I knew what he would find in town. I have been there myself, long ago. For months you had refused him; I thought he would seek satisfaction elsewhere. Yes—I tried to push him into doing so. The weather lies outside my grasp, but I can do more than conjure mere images in water.

Yes. I controlled you, too. I have your clothing, your hair, your tears. By their power I made you confront Mihal, masked and armed. I wanted you to see that men's promises of love cannot be trusted, that they will abandon us as soon as fidelity becomes a burden. This is how men *are*, my child. They lure us with sweet words, use us for their pleasure, discard us and our babes to be reviled forever after.

You may wish Mihal had given you the ring. You may think his defiance was foolish; you may claim you'd rather he surrender that ring and live. But it does not matter. Someday, that man will betray you. As I was once betrayed.

You will see. And then, my cursed daughter, you will come back to me.

You cannot trust him.

You cannot trust them.

You cannot *ever* trust them.

Any Rose My Mother Raised, Any Lane My Father Knows

I grew up inside three cages, each more subtle than the last. Two my parents built in order to keep me safe; the third was of their making, but not of their will. The ores from which its bars were forged were accident, disobedience, determination, love, but the metal with which they are wrought is a malice that will never die.

Two cages I have escaped so far, though my parents strove to keep me safe within. Now I must go, in defiance of their wishes, to confront the one who holds the final key.

The first of my cages, and the most obvious to see, was the one called Home.

Home was very small to begin with. In my infant years, it was my cradle or my parents' arms. They are and have always been loving; none can doubt that truth. No wet nurse had the suckling of me, and my nanny was there to lighten my mother's burden, not to take it away entire.

This was unusual, I found out later. My mother is a lady, of high enough wealth and rank that she might have rid her hands of any child-rearing had she wished it. Most ladies of her standing did. But I was forever in her hold, or if not there, no more than three steps away. *Too fond*, some of the servants said, clucking their tongues at the folly of their mistress—I heard this later, for of course my infant ears understood them not at the time. *She'll spoil that bairn, keeping it close like that.*

A few among them said other things, more quietly, where the

rest of their number could not hear. *She's afraid. Thinks if she lets the child out of her sight for a moment…and who's to say she's wrong?*

My father was less a part of my life, because he was more often away from home. He is a knight, and owes service to the king for that rank; he could not shirk it without giving offense. But when he was home, then often in his embrace I found myself, my chubby fingers reaching for his well-trimmed beard. This too was unusual, and I learned that sooner: few men of any sort, and fewer among knights, trouble themselves to do more than view their offspring from time to time, like a captain inspecting his troops. Thus assured of suitable health and growth, they return to their own business, which is not the raising of children.

The servants gossiped about this, too. My father feeding me, spoon in one sword-calloused hand, his shirt of fine cambric spotted with droplets of gruel. His delight in seeing my progress as I learned to grip, to roll over, to crawl across the floor. Never far from father or mother or both, never more than three steps away.

My tether grew as I did. Even the most doting of parents cannot remain so close to their child's side forever, and had they tried, I would have known much sooner that something was amiss. When I hauled myself to my feet and began to walk, Home's boundaries became those of our house. It is a fine snug manor, two storeys high—those stairs gave me great challenge in my early years, though now I take their steps two or three in a stride. But here, for the first time, I began to sense the bars of my cage, for I was forbidden to leave the house.

I thought little of this at first. It is the natural way of things for children to be subject to rules and bounds: I could enter the kitchen but not cross beyond the line of the great butcher-block, for past there lay the oven and stove, on which I might burn my hand. That was no part of the cage of which I speak, but rather simple caution…and indeed, like any high-spirited child, one day I ran where I should not, laid my hand where I should not, and reaped the consequences. My father was upset, my mother was angry, and all was as it would have been in an ordinary household.

But less ordinary was the way the doors and open windows

were forbidden to me. I minded very little when it was dark outside, for I feared the shadows without, and when the rain came
squalling down or the snow lay heavy on the ground there was
scant bait to tempt me out of the dry warmth of our manor. On
a fine summer day, though, with the sun bright and the breeze
carrying the intriguing scents of grass and growing flowers...

I could not be kept inside forever, any more than I could be
kept within three steps of father or mother or both. I would have
been a sickly child indeed had they kept me from the sun and fresh
air. Soon enough—I believe I was four years of age, or there-
abouts—the bars of the cage called Home were ready for me, and
I was at last permitted outside.

I did not find those bars straightaway. I was still young, and so
I did not venture far, only into the gardens that surrounded the
house. Behind the manor lie our vegetable gardens, laid in regimented beds and reeking at times of manure; here our servants
cultivate onions, carrots, marrows, and other things destined to
grace our tables. On the western side are herbs: comfrey, chamo-
mile, yarrow, and more, which my mother and her maids make
into tinctures and ointments for when we are ill. To the east lie
the stables.

But it was the southern side that became my favorite haunt,
for there my mother grows her roses.

She loves all kinds of flowers, but roses above all. Everything
from great showy blooms whose bushes require swaddling in
burlap when the weather turns cold to small, stubborn climbing
breeds whose tiny blossoms feel like a secret held close. Though
as carefully tended as the vegetable beds, the roses always felt
more wild to me. As soon as I was permitted outside I loved to
wander among them, even crawling along the ground to go where
no adult was small enough to follow. I came out with dirt all along
my front and tears all along my back where the thorns had caught
and cut, but my mother, laughing, said, "At least it's safe in there."
With the foolish naivete of a child, I thought she meant I could
not touch the stove from my prickly refuge.

The true bars of my cage, though, were not the gardens. Instead, this was my iron rule: I could roam where I pleased on the manor grounds, my parents decreed, so long as I did not go beyond the rowans.

These were planted all along the edges of our land, and I met them long before I knew it. My cradle was of rowan wood, though not from those trees, for they were too young to supply good timber. Above that cradle, too high for my infant arms to reach, a twig of rowan dangled from a red-dyed thread, and that did come from our trees. My father's walking-stick was cut from one of their branches, and my mother made their berries into jelly every year.

Past the gardens, past the stables, past the paddocks in which we exercised my parents' two fine riding horses and the two great cart horses that served the farms, the rowans marched in a regimented line, all around the manor grounds. A few were large, but most were small—for however quickly rowan grows, those trees were scarcely older than I was, having been planted shortly before my birth.

The cage called Home was barred with rowan wood. And when I was six, I was nearly lured outside it.

I did not mean to disobey.

I had grown old enough that I could roam quite well, and obedient enough that I was permitted out of my nurse's sight. In those days the grounds of our manor still seemed large to me, and I was happy to ramble along the rowan line, gazing out at what lay beyond.

Mostly that was farmland, with pasture interspersed. In those fields our tenants planted oats, rye, and wheat, or peas and beans in the years not given over to grains, and I liked to watch them move up and down the rows as they plowed and weeded and brought the harvest in. It was less interesting in the years when a field lay fallow, resting from the hard work of producing crops, for then there was nothing to see.

Even had the fields to the west not been fallow the autumn I was six, I would have eventually wandered along the shores of the burn that day. It is my favorite part of our lands after the rose garden, for here some trees have been permitted to remain that are not rowans. The result is a shaded little grove perpetually graced with music, the trickle of the burn over the rocks that form its bed. When I was young, I spent long hours sitting within the bounds of the rowans, tossing pebbles or sticks into the water, seeking to make the biggest splash I could or placing silent bets on the course a stick would follow as it floated away.

But when I came to it that day, there was something new.

The bank plunged steeply from the rowans down to the water's edge, and here and there exposed roots stood out from the earth like knees indecently bared. Caught among them was something shining and bright: a ball that seemed made of pure gold.

So busy was I gawping at it that I did not hear the woman until she spoke.

"Oh, at last—I've been hoping someone would come along!"

Tall, she was, even to one who saw not with the eyes of a child. Tall, and slender, and very gracious; I thought first of my mother, the only lady I knew. Certainly this woman must be a lady, for her gown was of fine green silk and the band that caught back her red hair was pure gold. No servant or farmwife dressed that way. And her voice was musical, sweet, as if every word she spoke were to be savored, no matter how banal.

"You're a fine young lad," she said to me, and curtsied just as if I were a laird. "What is your name?"

Six years old and obedient enough to be let out of sight, but in those days my manners were distinctly lacking. My mother and nurse had done their best to teach me courtesy, but when I hardly ever saw a stranger, I had little chance to practice those graces. In hindsight, I am glad of it: my rudeness may have saved me.

Not answering her, I merely stared, my gaze equally torn between the lady and the gleaming ball below. "What's that?" I asked.

When my attention turned once more to her, she dimpled with

an embarrassed smile. "That's my ball. I was walking along the top of the bank here, tossing it for amusement, and it fell from my hand. Before I could do anything, it rolled all the way down and across the stream and caught in those roots there. I wanted to fetch it, but…"

She had no need to finish her sentence. Beneath the hem of her silken gown peeped the toes of golden slippers; skirt and slippers alike would be ruined by a slide down the muddy bank to the burn, and if she tried to cross the rocks of the bed she might fall. No lady would risk it.

I squinted at the ball. It had rolled a surprisingly far distance up the bank on my side before catching in the roots—I remember thinking so, that it was surprising, though it never occurred to me to follow on to the next thought. Of course it was no accident that the ball had come to be caught there.

My heart was as torn as my gaze. To retrieve the ball, I would have to pass the line of rowans, and this I had promised not to do. Promises, as my nurse and mother and father alike had told me, were sacred.

But they had also told me it was noble to help someone in need, and with my father a knight and my mother a laird's daughter, did I not have a duty to uphold? Though my heart was not inclined to disobedience—not back then—I tried to reason my way to a resolution. Yes, I had sworn not to go beyond the rowans, but perhaps by that my parents only meant I should not go too far. They did not want me wandering out into the fields where I might get in the way of farmers, much less farther still, as a child's whimsy might lead. To retrieve the ball, though, I had only to slip between two rowans and slide a few feet down the bank. I needn't even put my feet in the water. I could balance on the roots, pry the ball free, toss it to—no, wipe it clean first on my sark, *then* toss it to the lady. A quick scramble up the bank and I would be back where I belonged, never having gone more than ten feet past where I should. No one would think anything of it if I came home a little muddy. I wouldn't even have to say what had happened.

No. Honesty was also noble, and though I have broken that

principle many times in my life—and intend to break it far more before I am done—to my six-year-old self, the proper course would be to confess my sins. When they heard my reasons, my parents and nurse would understand; or if they did not, I would take my punishment with stoicism and know in the future how I should interpret that rule.

The lady was watching me. "Oh, please," she said, her voice sweeter than ever, "my fine strong lad, will you help me? For the ball is very precious, not only for its gold but for the sentiment it holds, and I would very much hate to lose it."

I made up my mind. Noble aid, noble honesty, and if need be, noble stoicism. Better that than to act a churl.

Between two rowans, down a little edge of bank that almost formed a path, cling to the roots so I would not slip into the burn, and retrieve the ball. I could see it in my mind's eye, and I had bravely set forth when I heard my father's cry.

"*Stop!*"

Obedience was a habit deeply engrained. With my leading foot between two rowans, I stopped.

My father's arms came hard around my waist, slinging me behind him like a sack of flour. I was so startled I didn't even cry out. "Begone!" he thundered at the lady across the stream. "You are not welcome here!"

Her laugh was still sweet, but now it carried a poisonous edge. "I never thought I was. You have hidden yourself well, my erstwhile knight; it has taken me until now to find you. But now that I have…do you think you can keep your son safe from me?"

"I can and I will," my father said grimly, while I clambered to my feet and stared from behind the safety of his hip.

"For now, perhaps," the lady said, drawing herself upright. She seemed even taller, and the gold in her hair shone with its own light. "But I am patient. Can you keep him safe forever?"

She did not wait for an answer. Without me quite seeing how, between one blink and the next, she was gone, as if she had never been.

I sensed the bars of my second cage that day, when my father refused to answer any questions about who the lady had been and where she had gone. But in truth, they had surrounded me since the moment I was born.

My mother is a lady, my father a knight; this much I have always known. But they are strangers to the region, my maternal grandfather's lands lying far away. Nothing to remark upon in that—it is common for women to leave their homes when they wed—but of kin, my father seemed to have none. The estate on which we live came into our keeping by some means I still do not know, even now, when so many of my other questions have been answered.

The estate does not matter. The rest of it, however, matters a great deal.

Living where we do, with me confined so close to home, I had little opportunity to play with other children. For companionship I had my nurse, a series of hounds, and one scar-faced cat who lived in our barn. I did not know, because I was not meant to know, that my parents chose our servants carefully; they gave preference to the unmarried and the old, those with no young children of their own. On another estate I would have the servants' sons and daughters to play with, and those from the surrounding farms. But these were kept far from me, and our reputation suffered as a result.

Standoffish, many in the neighborhood said, placing the blame on my mother's shoulders. *Puts on airs, her being from the east and all—her bairn too good for the likes of ours.* My father escaped most of the censure, because the ways of the household were a woman's domain. Had those whisperers spoken to my mother, though, they would have known airs were the furthest thing from her nature.

Uncanny, said others. *Where did they come from, those two and their child? She's from the east, but him? Who are his people? And why do they keep so much to themselves?*

That struck far nearer the mark.

I heard these whispers when we went into the village, which we began to do after the incident at the stream. Or rather I should say that I began to do it, because until then I had never set foot outside our estate. That contributed to the whispers, for people in those parts did not take it well when a child failed to go to church. Every Sunday my mother had gone, and my father when he was at home, but never me.

It shocked me to be permitted this new liberty, so hard on the heels of my near disobedience. I had expected punishment, but received none, apart from a stern lecture; it was made clear to me that *not beyond the rowans* was meant very strictly, rather than in the general sense I had assumed. Not one fingertip, not one toe should pass their bounds. But once lecture was done, my father admonished me to be wary of all strangers and then closeted himself with my mother for private conference. When they emerged, they announced that I was to go to church with them next Sunday—leaving the confines of Home for the first time.

The lane beyond our gate might have been another country, so exotic did it seem to me. I walked between my parents, who never troubled to ride the short distance into the village—those who accused my mother of airs should have taken that into account. My father sang psalms as we walked, his voice deep and fine, and my mother instructed me in what I must know to behave properly in church.

The tail end of her instruction was overheard as we approached, by a red-faced woman carrying one babe in her arms and trailing another who held tight to her skirt. She moved her free hand in a gesture I recognized, though I had never been to church: the sign of the cross, as if to ward my family away.

Not my family. Me. Her gaze skittered off me like water off a hot pan, and she hurried ahead through the church doors.

She was not the only one to behave oddly around me, but then, I suppose I behaved oddly around them, too. *Be wary of strangers,* my father had said, but now everyone save the party from our estate was a stranger. The interior of the church was dim and the service was in a language I did not understand, and so I could not help fidgeting and peering around, which did not improve matters any. "Faerie child doesn't know what to do in God's house," I heard someone mutter, but I could not see who.

When the service ended, my parents ordered me to remain inside while they spoke to the priest. I did not need to be told that this was like the rowans: not one fingertip, not one toe should cross the threshold of the church until they came back.

They said nothing, however, of eavesdropping.

I was an honest child at heart, and so it took me a little while to screw up the courage to creep toward the door through which they'd vanished. I knew the principles of our faith, even if its ceremonies were new to me, and misbehavior in front of the rood seemed exceptionally wrong. But as I've said, I had begun to sense the bars of my second cage, and eventually curiosity drove me forward.

"—cannot disagree in principle," the priest was saying. "Your bairn's near enough the age for it, and it would go some way toward quieting the rumors about your family."

"But you have reservations," my father said, his voice a low, weary rumble.

"You know well I do. I had them six years ago, and nothing since then has sent them away."

"Not even this incident?" my mother said sharply.

"My lady, it isn't your reasoning I doubt, nor even the benefit. But what God will make of all we have done?" His sigh felt like it gusted beneath the door to chill my ankles. "Most days I regret that ever I did what you asked of me. But then you come in and tell me of this creature with her golden ball, and all those tales of your own past, yours and your husband's…they gleam with new truth. And I can only pray that God will approve of protecting an innocent soul, however it may be done."

My father said, "Then we are agreed," and I had the wit to scamper back from the door before they could find me with my ear pressed to its old boards.

All the tales of your own past. I did what you asked of me. Children of tender years are accustomed to knowing very little, but even then, I understood.

The bars of my second cage were made of secrets, and from

that day forth, I began to test them.

One secret was revealed immediately: my parents had spoken to the priest about confirming me in our faith. Thereafter, and for the next year, I went to church every Sunday with my mother, and my father when he was at home, and afterward the priest instructed me in what I needed to know. In short order I went from a little heathen to a proper Christian child, well-schooled in all the rites I had missed out on before, and in my seventh year I took my first communion, which went some way toward quieting the village rumors about me—though not all the way.

"Mother," I asked once, with deliberate ingenuousness, "am I a faerie child?"

"Certainly not!" she answered me sharply. "Do you doubt that I am your mother, or your father your sire?" When I allowed that I did not, she asked, "And do you doubt that we are human, and good Christians besides?"

"No," I said, beginning to feel quite ashamed.

But my mother's ire was not for me. "Tell me who has spoken ill of you, and I will see they do it no more."

Even at that age I knew it was not admirable to carry tales. "I cannot remember," I said, which was true after a fashion; I'd heard the whisper in an array of voices, and did not know who all of them belonged to.

The difficulty with breaking out of my second cage was that only two people truly held the key: my mother and my father, and neither of them would speak of what I wished to know. Who was that woman I'd seen down by the burn? Was she a queen my father had once served, that she called him her erstwhile knight? Why did we live so far away from any other kin? Why was I not permitted the society of other children? For even once I began attending church, even after I took the body and blood of our Lord from the priest, my mother frowned upon me playing with others in the village. One hot summer day a few of the boys invited me to the millpond, where they intended to swim, and you would have thought they wanted me to join them in baiting a wolf.

"But why may I not?" I asked, thinking longingly of that pond and its cool waters. There was no place at home where I could swim; even the burn was too shallow, and it lay beyond the rowans besides.

My mother clicked her tongue. "Because I don't want you to drown. You don't know how to swim."

"Yes, and I will never learn if I never try," I said, in what seemed to me a very reasonable voice. I was about ten at that point, I think, and starting to be wilful.

All the wilfulness in the world would have done me no good. "Boys like that," my mother said, leading me back home, "are not kind, even when they feign otherwise. No doubt once they had you there, they would have ducked you into the pond and held you under, to prove how strong they are."

I thought them no stronger than me, and in my heart I suspected my mother truly feared what the boys might say to me. I questioned the villagers in brief snatches, whenever I had the chance, and from them I gleaned a few hints amid the chaff of silly rumor: that scandal had chased my parents west, to this estate so far from either of their people. That I had been born much less than nine months after their wedding, which would certainly supply the scandal. That my father had no people anymore, at least none that would acknowledge him as their own—which seemed odd to me, if he were a knight trusted by the king, but I knew little of such things.

Of the lady who had tempted me by the burn, I gleaned only this, which my heart already knew: that she was no Christian woman, and perhaps no woman at all.

But in my thirteenth year, matters changed. From the east came riding a lady very different from the one I'd met that day, plump and weathered and graying at the temples. Although I'd been taught to be wary of strangers, my mother embraced this one and introduced her to me as my aunt, her elder sister. She was made a guest at our manor, the first we'd ever had.

By then I was old enough to be cunning. My father was absent, away on the king's business, and my mother could not be with her sister at all times. No doubt she cautioned our guest to be sparing in what she said to me…but surely, I thought, this woman knew things, and I might persuade her to speak of them.

My opportunity came on another fine autumn day, not much different the one seven years before when I met the lady along the burn. My aunt was out walking, and I contrived to slip away from the tasks I'd been given to meet up with her.

"Scandal? Oh yes," my aunt said, heaving a gusty sigh. "Your mother—I do not mean to speak ill of her, but she was always a disobedient, wilful girl. It's a wonder she bore a son as well behaved as you, given how you were conceived."

I affected shame and contrition. "Then it's true, what they say in the village? I was conceived out of wedlock?"

"That and more," my aunt said ominously. "I'm glad you came to me, boy; it's time you knew the truth of yourself. I cannot believe your parents have raised you in such ignorance."

To begin with I could not believe my luck, that she unfolded her tale so readily. Then I was astonished, then horrified. She told me of my mother's disobedience, going to a place forbidden to all young women, meeting my father—a disreputable man—and lying with him unwed. Getting herself with child, and disgracing the whole family with it. "She invented some absurd tale," my aunt said with a self-righteous sniff. "Rescuing your father from some faerie queen, him a captive for seven years—utter nonsense, which I can hardly even recall now."

At that I felt as if I came half out of my body. We were very close to the burn now, our paths having wended in that direction without me noticing. Where I had seen the lady my parents would not speak of.

My aunt was still talking. "Our father would have been within his rights to cut her off without a single shilling. Certainly your own father's people want nothing to do with him now! I suppose it's for the best that your parents chose to move away. But we've heard such odd rumors about how you're being raised out here, and with your grandfather doing poorly as he gets older, he insisted I come to see if I can't talk sense into your mother…"

Her words trailed off. Because we had come to the edge of the burn, and the lady was there once more, unchanged from seven years before. She curtsied to my aunt, but there was nothing of courtesy in it; only mockery. "I thank you for your service," she said. "The boy would never have listened to me, but to the first kin he meets? You were only too eager to help."

My aunt bristled at the condescension in her tone. "Help? I am afraid I do not know you, goodwife."

That address was a calculated insult, for no goodwife ever dressed as that lady did. She only smiled, like a predator sighting its prey. "I may not be able to come near the child's parents, since they won their freedom from me, but you are another matter. And you were only too eager to gossip with your father's guest this April past, who told you so much about your strangely isolated nephew."

Silence, as my aunt's jaw slipped loose from its firm line.

The lady in green silk turned her attention to me. "And you, my fine boy. How long can you live in your cage of rowan, leaving only on Sundays when I cannot seek you out? Will you bring a wife within these bars, never telling her you are hunted by a faerie queen? I have the patience of an immortal, boy. Whether it is this year or seventy years from now, *I will have you.*"

Then she turned and walked toward the nearest tree, a hawthorn with a bushy crown. She walked toward it, and then she was gone, faded away into the green.

My third cage is the malice of a faerie queen, and from that one, my parents cannot loose me. All they can do is protect me, and it is as the lady said: that cannot last forever.

If I am to live—if they are to be free of the shadow that still hangs over them, the vengeance vowed when they slipped the faerie's grasp—then I must take action myself.

The disappearance of the lady that day shocked my aunt into

silence. Remembering how my father had behaved seven years before, I feared what might happen if my mother heard aught of our encounter. I thought it very likely my parents would make me take holy vows, live out the remainder of my life behind sanctified walls no faerie could ever breach.

And so I swore my aunt to secrecy. She was only too glad to comply, fearing her own consequences should her sister discover she'd let loose so many secrets. In exchange for not betraying her, I extracted a few more things: every detail she could recall of my mother's "absurd tale," what lore she knew regarding faeries.

The rest, I have discovered for myself. Why I have never been permitted to play with other children. Why the priest fears God's judgment for his deeds. I have not come by this knowledge honestly; it has required a great deal of sneaking and lying, some of it even inside the church. But if my second cage is made of secrets, then truth is the sword with which I cut its bars apart—and the shield with which I will defend myself against the faerie queen.

I am prepared. It has been two years since that second encounter by the burn, and I cannot wait any longer; already my tenuous situation is falling apart. I am not a child, and there are expectations for a knight's son, none of which I can fulfill. If I am to act, it must be now.

I slipped away this morning, before dawn, going past the rowans on a Friday, when it is forbidden for me to leave Home. I thought the lady might come for me right then, but had a second plan if she did not. In the grey and uncanny light of a foggy morn, I went widdershins around the village church, like Burd Ellen in the tale.

The world spun. And when I opened my eyes, I found myself on a green hillside.

"And so," the faerie queen says with vast amusement, "you have delivered yourself into my hands. How practical of you."

Her court stands arrayed around us, creatures as thin as mist and as gnarled as trees. I keep my gaze fixed on the lady and my back very straight. "I come to offer you a trade," I say.

Her laugh is high and cold. "Why should I take anything you offer, when I already have what I want?"

"But can you keep it?" I ask. "My mother held onto my father when you transformed him into a serpent, a lion, a burning brand, all to win him free of you. Do you think she will do less for her only child?"

The lady's mouth thins. She knows I am right. Even now, I suspect, my mother is searching for me. She knows the tale of Burd Ellen, too; I must be quick if I am not to find her here at my side.

"Meet my conditions," I say, "and I will not cooperate with my mother nor my father nor any of my kin, if they try to take me from you."

"As you have reminded me, you are her son," the lady says, sweetly venomous. "You may try to escape yourself."

My hand to my heart, I say, "On my honor as the son of a knight, I will break no pact I make with you."

Her chin goes up as she considers me. Then she says, "Name your conditions."

I cannot stop the flick of my tongue across my dry lips, but it should be no surprise to her that I am nervous. "My mother loves her rose garden second only to my father and me. In exchange for me delivering myself into your hands, promise neither you nor yours will bring harm nor blight to any rose she has raised."

"I swear it," the lady says at once.

My heart beats faster. "My father travels a great deal in his duties. In exchange for me delivering myself into your hands, promise neither you nor yours will bring hindrance nor peril upon any lane that he knows."

"I swear it," the lady says again, and a smile begins to curve her perfect mouth.

I clasp my hands behind my back, for they are shaking and I do not want her to see. "My third condition is this: that your vengeance ends. Once our bargain is sealed, neither you nor yours will strike at my parents, nor any of their living or lawfully wedded kin, nor any child or grandchild or other descendant of their line henceforth."

The lady's smile grows wide and fierce. "I can be generous as well as cruel. In recompense for the loss of their son, I will not only do as you say; I will bless your parents with a daughter, and she and all who come from her will be safe from me. I swear it."

Relief breaks over me like a wave. Though my voice shakes like my hands, I manage to say, "Then our bargain is struck—and so I take my leave of you."

Utter silence descends. In this uncanny place, there is not even any wind. I can hear with perfect clarity as the faerie queen whispers, "*What?*"

I cannot hold back my own smile. "Here I stand before you: the child of Janet Carter and Thomas Lane, raised a boy, but baptized Rose Mary Lane." My voice firms, even rises to a shout. "I am a rose my mother raised; I am a lane my father knows; and I am the daughter you pledged to bless them with. I have delivered myself into your hands today, but by your own pledge, you have no claim on me!"

The lady rises to her feet in a storm of fury. Her courtiers break into snarls and roars—but mixed with it is shrill laughter. For there are some among faerie kind who respect a well-crafted trick, even when one of their own is its target.

I turn and walk away. This is the one thing I could not confirm, before I came here, but it is as I hoped: either keeping me in the faerie land would constitute hindrance or peril, or the lady has no wish to lay eyes on me ever again. I walk, and I come out in the ordinary grey light of a foggy morn, into the graveyard that lies beside the church.

My parents are there, clutching each others' hands so hard that all the blood has been pressed from them. It rushes back at the sight of me, but they stand frozen, hardly breathing.

My mother whispers, "Are you—did you—"

"I am free of her," I say simply, and then nothing more as their arms squeeze all my breath away.

I do not know what will happen after this. Whether I will go on as their son, despite the fear that someone will find me out, or live instead as their daughter, despite all the difficulties that will bring. Winning one's freedom from a faerie queen brings new troubles of its own, as my parents know all too well.

But as we leave the churchyard, I realize something. My parents were waiting for me there—waiting, not pursuing. They were not walking widdershins to come after me, to save their child as my mother once saved my father. Not because they love me any less, but because they knew I was no longer a child, and I must win this contest for myself.

Only then could I be truly free.

The Ballad of Tam Lin and Mulan

"Oh I compel you, brave sons a',
    Who honour your emperor well,
to come and join my bright army,
    The wild Hu to fell."

Mulan's brither is o'er young;
    He cannae ging tae war;
Mulan's faither is o'er auld;
    He cannae ride sae far.

Mulan has shortened her silk robe
    A little aboon her knee,
An' she has cut off her black cloud-hair
    A little aboon her bree,
And she's away to the army camp
    As fast as she can hie.

When she arrived at the army camp
    Tam Lin had her command,
And there she found his steed standing,
    But he was nae at hand.

She had nae ta'en a shining sword,
    A sword but only one,
When up then started bold Tam Lin,
    Says, Soldier, thou seems sae young.

Thou lacks the merest hint o' beard,
    So why lifts thou the sword?
Or why comes thou to this far war-front
    To serve thy highborn laird?

My faither, he is too auld tae serve,
    And my brither's younger still;
I'll fight and die as ony man
    Against all those who wish us ill.

Mulan has shortened her silk robe
    A little aboon her knee,
An' she has cut off her black cloud-hair
    A little aboon her bree,
And she's away to the battlefield
    As fast as she can hie.

Four and twenty soldiers strang
    were training well for war,
And oot then came the brave Mulan,
    The slightest o' them a'.

Four and twenty soldiers strang
    Were fighting in the fray,
And oot then came the brave Mulan,
    In battle boldly played.

Oot then spake an auld gray man,
    Lay o'er the fortress wa',
and says, "Alas, for thee, Mulan,
    But we'll be killed a'.

"Haud your tongue, ye auld fac'd man,
    Some ill death may ye die!
I'd stand all year in the front-most rank
    If there I might see thee."

Out then spake her sergeant bold,
    And he spake frank and free,
"An' aye alas, Mulan," he said,
    "Tae win needs mair than ye."

"If I am no' enough," she said,
    "Which I cannot gainsay,
We'll need a clever stratagem
    If we're tae win the day.

"The Hu will ne'er break nor run
    As they're a stalwart foe;
I wad nae gie my ain red blood
    For hope tae mak them go.

"Wi' horses they are well-supplied,
    And likewise well wi' meat;
Tae mak' them go back whence they cam'
    Will be nae little feat."

Mulan has shortened her silk robe
    A little aboon her knee,
And she has cut off her black cloud-hair
    A little aboon her bree,
And she's away to the army camp
    As fast as she can hie.

When she returned tae army camp
    Tam Lin had her command,
And there she found his steed standing,
    But he was nae at hand.

She had nae ta'en a shining sword,
    A sword but only one,
When up then started bold Tam Lin,
    Says, "Soldier, thou seems sae young.

"Why dost thou spy on me, Mulan,
    And search wi'in ma tent,
Unless it is because ye fear
    I haee some ill intent?"

"Oh tell me, tell me, Tam Lin," she says,
    "For a' the blood we've shed,
If e'er ye've been loyal to
    The men that ye have led?"

"In past years I lived i' the north
    All wi' my wife and child,
And ance it cam' the town was sacked
    By mounted warriors wild.

"And captive we were taken a',
    Me wi' my wife and son,
Tae serve as slaves the warrior Hu
    That had the battle won;
An' there was much o' cruelty then,
    O' mercy there was none.

"The general o' the Hu forces
    Told me tae go and spy,
Ay if I worked on his behalf,
    Then he would spare their lives,
But if I proved a traitor, then
    My wife and child would die.

"But if ye come wi' me, Mulan,
    Then we can set them free,
And then I'll turn against the Hu
    And northward they will flee.

"We'll ride away i' dark of night
    And go seek oot the town;

Ye'll climb the walls wi' silent speed
    An' throw a rope back doon."

"But how can we twa bring them oot
    If they are held sae tight?
And how can we return tae camp
    Afore the end of night?"

"We'll dress oorselves in darkest robes
    An' black oor faces too;
Wi' padding on oor strang boot-soles
    We'll leave nae print as clue.

"Betwixt the circuits o' the guards
    We'll slip intae the keep;
A potion strang wi'in their wine
    Will send them a' tae sleep.

"The first cell-door we'll open quick
    Tae save my son from strife;
The second lock will nae stand fast
    Between me an' my wife;
Then softly, softly, oot we'll gae
    For sake o' a' their life.

"But they'll be weak with prison lang
    And will nae run sae fast;
It's up to ye, Mulan the brave,
    The gate tae get us past.

"By shadowed paths we'll hae tae ging,
    Awa' frae a' the guards,
Or lead them off so they wilnae see
    When we must cross their yards.

"By trickery ye must keep us safe

If ony come too near,
Oh, cast a stone to make a sound
 And so deceive their ears.

"With knife an' sword ye'll hae tae fight
 If we come tae be caught—
Strike hard and true as e'er ye have
 In ony battle fought.

"At last we'll come unto the gate
 Which ye must open wide,
Then we'll mount on oor horses swift
 And hame tae safety ride."

Gloomy, gloomy was the night
 And dangerous was the way,
As Mulan and Tam Lin i' stealth
 Tae foeman's camp did gae.

Aboot the middle o' the night
 They saw the fortress wall;
These warriors were hot wi' hope
 To see the Hu force fall.

They dressed themselves in darkest robes
 And blacked their faces too;
Wi' padding on their strang boot-soles
 They left nae print as clue.

Sae weel she minded whit he said,
 They fled wi'out a scratch;
Not one among the enemy
 Tam Lin and kin could catch.

Out then spak Hu's general
 From top his fortress wall:

"Them that came in dark o' night
  Have stolen away my thralls.

Out then spak Hu's general
  And an angry man was he:
"Shame betide her ill-far'd face,
  And an ill death may she die,
Mulan has ta'en my loyal spy
  And turned him against me.

"But had I kent, Tam Lin," he says,
  "What noo this night I see,
I wad hae killed him at the start
  Not left him fighting free."

Song lyrics

Because these are traditional songs, there are *many* different versions of the lyrics for each one. I've chosen ones that come the closest being to the versions I know, without being taken from those specific recordings (since I'm not sure in all cases whether those lyrics are taken from a public domain source or are specific to that artist).

⧉

"Tam Lin"

I forbid you maidens all that wear gold in your hair
To travel to Carter Haugh, for young Tam Lin is there.

Them that go by Carter Haugh, but they leave him a pledge
Either their mantels of green or else their maidenhead.

Janet tied her kirtle green a bit above her knee
And she's gone to Carter Haugh as fast as go can she.

She doth pull the double rose, a rose but only two
And up then came young Tam Lin, says lady pull no more.

And why come you to Carter Haugh without command from me
I'll come and go, young Janet said, and ask no leave of thee.

Janet tied her kirtle green a little bit above her knee
And she's gone to her father as fast as go can she.

Then up spoke her father dear, and he spoke meek and mild
Well alas Janet, he said, I think you go with child.

Well if that be so, Janet said, myself shall bear the blame
There's not a knight in all your halls shall get the baby's name.

For if my love were an earthly knight, as he is an elfin grey
I'll not change my own true love for any knight you have.

Janet tied her kirtle green a bit above her knee
And she's gone to Carter Haugh as fast as go can she.

Oh tell to me Tam Lin she said, why came you here to dwell
The Queen of Fairy's caught me when from my horse I fell.

And at the end of seven years she pays a tithe to hell
I so fair and full of flesh am feared it is myself.

But tonight is Halloween and the fairy court rides
Those that would let true love win, At Miles' Cross they must hide.

First let pass the horses black and let pass the brown
Quickly run to the white steed and pull the rider down.

For I ride on the white steed, the nearest to the town
For I was an earthly knight, they give me that renown.

They will turn me in your arms to a newt or a snake
Hold me tight and fear not, I am your baby's father.

And they will turn me in your arms into a lion bold
Hold me tight and fear not and you will love your child.

And they will turn me in your arms into a naked knight
Cloak me in your mantle and keep me out of sight.

And in the middle of the night she heard the bridle ring
She heeded what he did say and young Tam Lin did win.

Then up spoke the fairy queen, an angry queen was she
Who betide her ill-farr'd face, an ill death may she die.

Oh had I known Tam Lin, she said, what this night I did see
I'd have looked him in the eye and turned him to a tree.

⚬

"The Twa Magicians"

The lady sits at her own front door as straight as the willow wand,
And by there come a lusty smith with his hammer in his hand

CHORUS
  Bide, lady, bide, for there's nowhere you can hide,
  For the lusty smith will be your love, and he will lay your pride.

"Why may you sit there, lady fair, all in your robes of red?
Why, come tomorrow at this same time, I'll have you in my bed."

"Away, away, you coal-black smith, would you do me this wrong,
For to think to have my maidenhead that I have kept so long?
I'd rather I was dead and cold, and my body laid in the grave,
Than a husky, dusky, coal-black smith my maidenhead should have."

So the lady she curled up her hand, and she swore upon the mould
That he'd not have her maidenhead for all of a pot of gold.
But the blacksmith he curled up his hand, and he swore upon the
  mass

That he would have her maidenhead for the half of that or less

So the lady, she turned into a dove and flew up into the air,
Ah, but he became an old cock-pigeon, and they flew pair and pair

So the lady, she turned into a mare as dark as the night was black,
Ah, but he became a golden saddle, and he clung upon to her
    back

So the lady, she turned into a hare, and ran all over the plain,
Ah, but he became a greyhound dog, and he ran her down again

So the lady, she turned into a fly and fluttered up into the air,
Ah, but he became a big hairy spider and dragged her into his lair

So the lady, she turned into a sheep a-grazing on yon common,
Ah, but he became a big horny ram, and soon he was upon her

So she turned into a full-dressed ship, and she sailed all over the sea,
Ah, but he became a bold captain and aboard of her went he

So the lady, she turned into a cloud a-floating away in the air,
Ah, but he became a lightning flash and he zipped right into her

So she turned into a mulberry tree, a mulberry tree in the wood,
Ah, but he came forth as the morning dew and he sprinkled her
    where she stood

So the lady, she ran into the bedroom, and she changed into a bed,
Ah, but he became a green coverlet and he gained her maiden-head

And once she woke, he took her so, and still he bade her bide,
And the lusty smith became her love, for all of her mighty pride.

"The Unquiet Grave"

The wind doth blow tonight, my love
A few small drops of rain
I never had but one true love
In cold clay she is lain

I'll do as much for my true love
As any young man may
I'll sit and mourn upon her grave
A twelvemonth and a day

The twelvemonth and a day being up
A voice spoke from the deep
Who is it sits and weeps upon my grave
And will not let me sleep

'Tis I, 'tis I, thy own true love
That weeps upon thy grave
Until I have one kiss from your cold lips
No comfort will I have

My lips are cold as clay, my love
My breath is earthy strong
And had you one kiss from my cold lips
Your time would not be long

Down in yonder garden gay
Love, where we used to walk
The sweetest flower that ever I saw
Is withered to a stalk

The stalk is withered dry, my love
So will our hearts decay
So hold yourself content, my love
Till death calls you away

☙

"John Barleycorn"

There were three men come out of the west
Their fortunes for to try
And they have made a solemn vow
John Barleycorn must die

They plowed him in three furrows deep
Laid clods all on his head
And they have made a solemn oath
John Barleycorn was dead

Well then there came a shower of rain
Which from the clouds did fall
John Barleycorn sprang up again
And so amazed them all

Well then came men with great sharp scythes
To cut him off at the knee
They bashed his head against a stone
And they used him barbarously

Well then came men with great long flails
To cut him skin from bone
The miller has used him worse than that
He ground him between two stones

They wheeled him here, they wheeled him there
Wheeled him into the barn
And they have used him worse than that
They bunged him in a vat

They worked their will upon John Barleycorn

But he lives to tell the tale
We pour him into an old brown jug
And we call him home-brewed ale

∽

"Tom O'Bedlam" or "Bedlam Boys"

For to see Mad Tom of Bedlam
Ten thousand miles I traveled
Mad Maudlin goes on dirty toes
For to save her shoes from gravel.

Still I sing bonny boys, bonny mad boys
Bedlam boys are bonny
For they all go bare and they live by the air
And they want no drink or money.

I now repent that ever
Poor Tom was so disdain-ed
My wits are lost since him I crossed
Which makes me thus go chained

I went down to Satan's kitchen
For to get me food one morning
And there I got souls piping hot
All on the spit a-turning

There I took up a caldron
Where boiled ten thousand harlots
Though full of flame I drank the same
To the health of all such varlets

My staff has murdered giants
My bag a long knife carries

For to cut mince pies from children's thighs
And feed them to the fairies

The spirits white as lightening
Would on me travels guide me
The stars would shake and the moon would quake
Whenever they espied me

No gypsy, slut or doxy
Shall win my mad Tom from me
I'll weep all night, with stars I'll fight
The fray shall well become me

And when that I'll be murdering
The Man in the Moon to the powder
His staff I'll break, his dog I'll shake
And there'll howl no demon louder

So drink to Tom of Bedlam
Go fill the seas in barrels
I'll drink it all, well brewed with gall
And maudlin drunk I'll quarrel

For to see Mad Tom of Bedlam
Ten thousand years I have traveled
Mad Maudlin goes on dirty toes
For to save her shoes from gravel.

❧

"The Twa Sisters" or "The Cruel Sister"

There were two sisters in one bower
Edinburgh, Edinburgh
There were two sisters in one bower

Stirling for aye
Ah, there were two sisters in one bower
And there came a knight to be their wooer
Bonny Saint Johnston stands upon Tay

Oh, he courted the eldest with glove and ring
But he loved the youngest above all things
Oh, the eldest, she was vexed full sore
And sore she envied her sister fair

And as it fell on one morning clear
The eldest came to her sister fair
Oh, sister, oh, sister, won't you walk down
And view the ships all sailing around

Oh, the youngest, she stood on the water's brink
And the eldest came and she pushed her in
Oh, she's took her by the middle so small
And she's broke her bonny back to the jaw

Oh, sister, oh, sister, lend me a hand
And you will be heir to half my lands
Oh, sister, oh, sister, I'll not lend me hand
I'll have your man and your houses and all of your land

Oh, sister, oh, sister, save my life
I swear I shall never be any man's wife
Oh, your cherry cheeks and your yellow hair
Make me go a maiden for ever more

Oh, sometimes she sank and sometimes she swam
Until that she came to the bonny mill dam
Oh, the miller's daughter was baking the bread
And she came out for water as she had need

Oh, father, father, there swims a swan

So now, won't you hasten and draw up your dam
Oh, the miller, he came and he drew up his dam
And there he saw the drowned woman

He laid down on the bank to dry
When the King's own harper, he passed by
Oh, he made a harp of her breastbone
Whose sounds would melt a heart of stone

And the strings he formed of her yellow hair
Whose notes made sad the listening ear
Oh, and he laid the harp down on a stone
And soon it began to play all alone

And the first tune it played was, me father the King
And the second it played was, me mother the Queen
Oh, and yonder stands my brother Hugh
And by him, my William, sweet and true

And the third tune it played was, me false sister Jean
So slyly she pushed me into the stream
Oh, and then up spoke her false sister Jean
Says, we'll pay this harper and have him be gone

Oh, but up then spoke her father the King
Says, we'll have the tune played over again
Well, they built a fire that would burn any stone
And in it they threw her false sister Jean

✳

"The Twa Corbies"

As I was walking all alane
I heard twa corbies making a mane:

The tane unto the tither did say,
'Whar sall we gang and dine the day?'

'—In behint yon auld fail dyke
I wot there lies a new-slain knight;
And naebody kens that he lies there
But his hawk, his hound, and his lady fair.

'His hound is to the hunting gane,
His hawk to fetch the wild-fowl hame,
His lady 's ta'en anither mate,
So we may mak our dinner sweet.

'Ye'll sit on his white hause-bane,
And I'll pike out his bonny blue e'en:
Wi' ae lock o' his gowden hair
We'll theek our nest when it grows bare.

'Mony a one for him maks mane,
But nane sall ken whar he is gane:
O'er his white banes, when they are bare,
The wind sall blaw for evermair.'

❧

"Sovay" or "The Female Highwayman"

Sovay, Sovay, all on a day
She dressed herself in man's array.
With a sword and pistol all by her side,
To meet her true love,
To meet her true love away did ride.

As she was riding over the plain,
She met her true love and bid him stand.

"Your gold and silver, kind sir," she said,
"Or else this moment,
Or else this moment your life I'll have."

And when she'd robbed him of his store,
She said, "Kind sir, there's just one thing more--
A golden ring which I know you have,
Deliver it,
Deliver it your sweet life to save."

"O, that golden ring a token is;
My life I'll lose, the ring I'll save."
Being tender-hearted just like a dove,
She rode away,
Rode away from her true love.

Next morning in the garden green,
Just like two lovers they were seen.
He spied his watch hanging by her cloak
Which made him blush,
Made him blush like any rose.

"O what makes you blush at so silly a thing?
I thought to have had your golden ring.
'Twas I that robbed you all on the plain,
So here's your watch
Here's your watch and your gold again.

"For I did intend and it was to know
If that you were my true love or no.
Well, now I have a contented mind;
My heart and all,
My heart and all my gear is thine."

Afterword

As evidenced by my earlier collections *A Breviary of Fire*, *Monstrous Beauty*, and *Never After: Thirteen Twists on Familiar Tales*, my work often draws from the well of folklore all over the world. But that isn't limited to the more familiar subjects of fairy tales and myths, and in fact, some of my favorite moments of inspiration have come while listening to songs.

Music actually has a huge influence on my writing. Both my novels and my short stories often have music I associate with them, which helps set the mood for a scene or a setting and jump-starts my thoughts back into the right headspace when I come back to work on it again. Most of what I listen to for that, however, is either instrumental music—I have a *large* library of film and TV scores—or else in languages I don't speak fluently enough for the words to be a distraction.

These stories largely came about via a different route, often involving me walking or driving somewhere. That's when I'm most likely to be listening to music in English, and when my brain is in the right sort of receptive, free-associating mode to say "hang on a sec." My thoughts snag on some inconsistency or plot hole in the lyrics, or I begin riffing on some idea they've inspired.

Which might be why, in recent years, I've written so many fewer of these. Most of the stories in this collection date back—at least in their original inspirations, if not their final, published forms—to my time in college and grad school, when I was often walking to class (and listening to music as I went). Since moving to California and writing full-time, I've been more of a homebody, and also folk music has become a smaller proportion of what's on regular rotation in my library.

But that doesn't mean I won't come back to this mode someday! Just that, should any song-based story ideas mug me in the future, you're more likely to see them mixed in with their more prose-based folkloric fellows.

And that concludes my general remarks. For commentary on the individual stories, turn the page.

Story Notes

Notes on "And Ask No Leave of Thee"

The funny thing about this story is, I wound up not even leveraging the idea that launched it into motion.

I don't remember why I started wondering if it were possible to do the transformation sequence from the end of the ballad in a non-magical fashion. The idea I came up with is the one you see here, where Tam Lin changes the image of himself in J's mind, rather than physically turning into a lion or a snake or a burning brand. It was easy to turn Janet's defiance and pregnancy out of wedlock from the ballad into an angry young woman making bad decisions at a nightclub, and a gang background could stand in for the faerie court, so I was all set to write a completely non-speculative rendition of "Tam Lin"!

…but what would I do with it?

I have always been a genre writer. Mostly fantasy, a bit of it dark enough to qualify as horror; a few things that border into science fiction; a tiny number of non-speculative historical pieces. But a mainstream story? I had no idea where to try and sell that.

Which is why, as I wrote my way through this story, I wound up deciding to put the magic back in. There's more going on than just street violence—but the street violence is still there, all the things I had in mind for the mundane version. J is still an angry young woman making bad decisions at a nightclub. Tam Lin still remains in human form, "transforming" himself through his confession of the awful things he's done. The Queen of Faerie is still essentially a gang leader. (She always has been.)

In many ways it's one of the darker stories I've written, even if it goes less overtly into horror. But I like how, in coming up with a non-magical approach, I prodded myself to reach somewhere less comfortable, more raw.

"And Ask No Leave of Thee" was originally published in *Neither Beginnings Nor Endings*, ed. Richard Fife, in April 2022.

NOTES ON "THEN BIDE YOU THERE"

I have a love-hate relationship with the song "The Twa Magicians."

In the versions I've heard, it is *super catchy* and fun to sing. And then you pay attention to *what* you're singing, and you realize this is a howlingly rape-y song about a man who refuses to take no for an answer. About how it's only "pride" that makes the woman refuse, and pride is a bad thing for her to have, so that gets forcibly taken away. The sexual imagery of the lyrics isn't even subtle.

So I had to write a version where she's allowed to keep the upper hand. As I told students once, when giving a talk on story inspiration, sometimes things are more hatefic than fanfic.

"Then Bide You There" was originally published in *Dream of Shadows* #4, in July 2022.

NOTES ON "VĪS DĒLENDĪ"

I spent *years* wanting to write a story based on the folksong "The Unquiet Grave." Over a decade, certainly, though I don't know when exactly it started. And had I leapt on that impulse right away, I would have written a fairly straightforward narrative based on the events of the lyrics, and with enough persistence, I probably could have managed to sell it somewhere, if not for very much money.

But for whatever reason, I didn't get around to writing it immediately. And by the time I came back to that idea, a straightforward retelling was no longer enough for me. I tried doing a kind of folkloric version, hoping that voice alone would suffice to carry me through, but it was sufficiently uninteresting that I quit after less than a page. There just wasn't enough *there* there. I told myself it belonged in the graveyard of story ideas not really worth writing—and I tried to bury it there, I really did! Yet my subconscious kept insisting it wanted to write something based on that song. To make that work, I needed more.

I needed a second song.

I haven't included the lyrics here, but the piece I was missing came from a song variously called "Flora" or "The Lily of the West" (or sometimes both of those together). That speaker in that one is a man who's been betrayed by his lover, Flora…

…or has he?

The song is all about how he still loves his "faithless Flora" even after she left him for another man (a man he then murders). But did Flora ever love him? Heck, in the version I was listening to, it was entirely possible that he never even *spoke* to Flora—that their relationship existed only in his mind.

Now *that* was a story.

The first version of which was absolutely terrible. I tried to stick with that folkloric voice while leaning into an unreliable narrator— the character who later became Harrik Neconnu—but it really, really didn't work. On the suggestion of a friend, I stepped away to a different style and went hard on the worldbuilding, and the result is what you read here!

"Vīs Dēlendī" was originally published in issue #27 of *Uncanny Magazine*, in March/April 2019. It also netted me my only Year's Best reprint to date, in *The Year's Best Science Fiction and Fantasy, 2020 Edition*, ed. Rich Horton.

NOTES ON "WHAT STILL ABIDES"

I remember being in graduate school, listening to Heather Alexander's rendition of "John Barleycorn." I'm not very good at picking up lyrics right away, so I'd heard the song several times before the final line of that version jumped out at me, a cheery declaration: "And we shall drink his blood!"

What the *hell* was I listening to?

I backed up to the beginning of the song and paid attention this time, and I soon realized the song was metaphorically about the brewing of beer. Oh, good; that was much less alarming. I went on my merry way and heard the song any number of times more, until one day my hindbrain whispered:

What if it wasn't *about that?*

I'm not sure what masochistic impulse made me decide this needed to be written in Anglish, a.k.a. English stripped of all words derived from non-Germanic languages, but "masochistic" is definitely the right descriptor for it. Some swaps are easy—"understand" instead of "comprehend"—but some are not: all of our words related to memory are non-Germanic, which is why I had to coin "old-thought" right there in the first line. For God's sake, *face* is derived from Latin. I literally had to go through the story word by word, looking each term up in the Oxford English Dictionary and hunting synonyms in the Oxford Historical Thesaurus, and I owe a debt of gratitude to Sara Bryan for helping me massage my sentence structure to be more authentically Anglo-Saxon-sounding.

It was a fun experiment, and I'm never doing it again.

"What Still Abides" was originally published in *Clockwork Phoenix 4*, ed. Mike Allen, in July 2013.

NOTES ON "MAD MAUDLIN"

If you've read much Mercedes Lackey—or even just seen enough of her works on the shelf—you've encountered the folksong "Tom o' Bedlam" or "Bedlam Boys" before. She thoroughly mined its lyrics for the titles of her Bedlam Bard novels, and I can't blame her, because they are *damned* evocative.

But there's not much of a story there. Just a long list of really vivid events without any context or through-line, apart from Maudlin seeking Tom. That, however, did hand me a character: Mad Maudlin herself. And the notion of her in modern times, folkloric weirdness colliding with psychiatric medicine, seemed really fruitful.

Figuring out how to thread the needle of this story, though, was a challenge. After all, our conception of and approach to "madness" is very different now from the days when Bethlehem Hospital was a notoriously awful mental asylum nicknamed *Bedlam*. I didn't want the story to be "Maud isn't mad, just connected to folklore," because the madness is baked into the core of the concept. But I also didn't want the story to be "Maud is mentally ill and there's no folklore going on." I wanted to—and tried to—hold both things as simultaneously true: she *is* insane—a literal embodiment of madness in the world—but also right about the things she sees.

That is, until Peter takes her place. Delusions are not so easily defeated.

I owe a *massive* debt of thanks to my husband, Kyle Niedzwiecki; his mother, Sandra Niedzwiecki; and most of all to my friend, Rachel Manija Brown, for lending their knowledge of psychology, psychiatry, and the therapeutic process to this story. Some stories you can write and then get fact-checked; this one needed consultation before I even began writing, to figure out what shape the story ought to have.

"Mad Maudlin" was originally published on *Tor.com*, in January 2021.

Notes on "Cruel Sisters"

I'm far from the first author to write something based on this folksong, because let's face it: a harp made of human bone and strung with a dead woman's hair is the kind of horrifically amazing image that just *begs* to be used again.

But in this instance, I'm actually inspired by a very specific version of the song. (Not the one quoted here in this book, for rights reasons.) In some renditions, the sisters are the daughters of a farmer; in others, they're the daughters of a lord or a king. Loreena McKennitt's recording is the only one I know that wanders randomly from the former to the latter in the course of the song, without explanation. And that got me thinking about the discrepancy between the different versions—a perfectly normal thing to have happen in folklore, of course, but what if it wasn't inconsistency? What if there was a story there?

The fact that it led me to write a retelling where the focus was more on revolution than on jealousy over a man was just a nice bonus.

"Cruel Sisters" was originally published in *Daily Science Fiction*, in March 2020.

Notes on "The Twa Corbies"

This is the one that started my mini-trend of writing stories based on folksongs, and I think the inspiration for it may actually date all the way back to high school.

For some unknown reason, the lyrics of this song were included in the poetry textbook we used in my senior year English class. Alas, I don't recall anymore whether the notes to that section are where someone first pointed out to me an oddity in the lyrics: the knight is "new-slain," and yet his lady has already "taken another mate"—at a point where the only people who know he's lying dead in a ditch are his hawk, his hound, and the lady in question. Smells like foul play to me…

I didn't do anything with that idea, though, until my senior year of college, when I'd finally learned how to write short fiction that was not an abject failure right out of the gate. Then the question of how the speaker in the song understood the ravens' speech (which, in typical folkloric fashion, is treated as irrelevant logistics) merged in my head with various mythical bits about people understanding the speech of birds, and I had my entry point into the story.

"The Twa Corbies" was originally published in issue #31 of

Talebones, in December 2005.

Notes on "Oh, My Cursed Daughter"

This story is both very old and much newer.

The very old part dates back almost as far as "The Twa Corbies," when I wrote a different version of this story and shopped it around for a while before ultimately trunking it. I've done that to fewer than a dozen stories in my career thus far; most of the time, I either know I've written something very mediocre and don't bother to send it out, or I believe in it enough to keep subbing until it sells. But in the six years it was on the market, I leveled up enough in my short fiction that this one felt really slight by comparison—plus, I'd spotted a problem with what I'd written.

In my head, that version of the story wasn't a comment on sexuality. The fact that the antagonist was magically manipulating everybody wasn't because she was a lesbian; it was because not admitting you're in love with your best friend can lead in bad directions. But the fact remained that it was a story with a lesbian character who was at best very manipulative, and at worst cruel to the point of evil. And I didn't want to put that out in the world.

So into the trunk it went. But the song stayed in my head, because I've always been compelled by its space alien logic: "If you'd given up that trinket I gave you instead of bravely accepting death, I would have murdered you!" (My husband has instructions to surrender any and all gifts I've ever given him if it's necessary to save his life.) Then one day I realized, I didn't have to completely change the structure of the story; I only had to change one kind of love to another. Instead of a best friend harboring secret romantic feelings, a mother trying to protect her daughter—a mother so scarred by her own past that she assumes the betrayal she suffered is inevitable for everyone. And instead of writing it from the perspective of the daughter, let us see that through the mother's eyes.

I like this version *much* better.

"Oh, My Cursed Daughter" was originally published in *Dream of Shadows*, in April 2023.

Notes on "Any Rose My Mother Raised, Any Lane My Father Knows"

Like many of the stories in this collection, the seed had been in my head a long time. "Tam Lin" hinges on Janet being pregnant; well, what happens with her child? Does the Queen of Faerie leave the kid alone? I've seen more than one version that suggests the answer will *not* be "yes." I thought there was great potential in doing a second generation story.

But I had no idea what that potential should be.

I wrote a bit less than a thousand words all the way back in 2005, hoping that if I just followed my fingers I'd wind up with a story. It stalled out completely. And that's where matters remained until an editor from *Frivolous Comma* approached me about writing something for what, at the time, was intended to be an anthology of stories about children (defined as anywhere up to late teens). I don't have any children, and that period of life isn't one that tends to compel my imagination, so it seemed like an awkward match—until I browsed through my false starts and list of ideas and realized, wait, I did have *one* that could very plausibly be about a teenager.

And because the anthology encouraged stories about the problems faced by children, I liked the idea of focusing on Janet's kid having to step out from under parental protection and deal with the Queen of Faerie directly. It took a lot of brainstorming, though, to decide what that confrontation would look like: saving some other true love in some other fashion? Seducing the Queen and turning it into a human/faerie romance? Fiddle contest, dragging in a completely different folkloric tradition?

No: *trickery*. The moment I lighted on the notion of telling the story in the first person, of obfuscation both in the narration and in the character's life of her true gender, of hinging everything off the double meaning of a name, I had an ending that felt like a proper victory.

"Any Rose My Mother Raised, Any Lane My Father Knows" was originally published in *Frivolous Comma* in August 2024.

Notes on "The Ballad of Tam Lin and Mulan"

You may very well be thinking, "What the heck *is* this?"

My usual habit in these collections is to include only stories (and, since *The Atlas of Anywhere*, poems) that have been previously published. In the case of this bonus poem, though, I never even attempted to submit it anywhere, because I'm all too aware that it looks really, really random. Why on earth did I decide I needed to mash up a Chinese source with a Scottish one?

The answer lies in work of Larry Hammer, a poet friend previously mentioned several times in the notes to *A Breviary of Fire* (he also contributed a poetry translation to my novel *The Game of 100 Candles*). He likes to translate both Japanese and Chinese poetry, and his rendition of one of the versions of the Mulan ballad included these lines:

She exchanges her fine silk gown,
She washes off her white face-powder:
She spurs her horse to the army tents,
With fervent sighs, takes sword in hand.

Which immediately chimed in my head with one version of the chorus of "Tam Lin":

Janet has kilted her green kirtle
    a little aboon her knee
And she has broded her yellow hair
    a little aboon her bree
And she's away to Carterhaugh
    as fast as she can hie.

And then I *had* to write the mashup—complete with consulting a friend who's a professor of Chinese linguistics to figure out whether there were in fact suitable characters to transliterate the name "Tam Lin," even though that transliteration wound up nowhere in the poem.

Is the result a little random? Oh, more than a little. To the point where I figured the odds of finding an editor who wanted to buy a really long mashup poem in Scots were so small you'd need a microscope to find them. But since this collection already contained two works based on "Tam Lin," it seemed a shame not to include it!

My thanks to Derek Muir and David Goodman for polishing the Scots in here! I didn't implement every single one of their suggestions, for the sake of readability to a broader audience, but their comments greatly improved the voice of this poem.

About the Author

MARIE BRENNAN is a former anthropologist and folklorist who shamelessly leans on her academic fields for inspiration. She recently misapplied her professors' hard work to *The Market of 100 Fortunes* and *The Waking of Angantyr*. She is the Hugo Award-winning and Nebula and World Fantasy-nominated author of the Victorian adventure series The Memoirs of Lady Trent along with several other series, over ninety short stories, several poems, and the New Worlds series of worldbuilding guides; as half of M.A. Carrick, she has written the Rook and Rose epic fantasy trilogy. For more infor-mation and social media, visit linktr.ee/swan_tower.

About Book View Café

Book View Café Publishing Cooperative (BVC) is an author-owned cooperative of professional writers, publishing in a variety of genres such as fantasy, romance, mystery, and science fiction.

BVC authors include New York Times and USA Today best-sellers; Nebula, Hugo, and Philip K. Dick Award winners; World Fantasy Award and Campbell Award nominees; and winners and nominees of many other publishing awards.

Since its debut in 2008, BVC has gained a reputation for producing high-quality e-books, and is now bringing that same quality to its print editions.